--- ★ ---

"Do you think she'd recognize you?"

I nodded. I didn't trust my voice.

"Try."

I moved to the side of her bed where she could see me. "Connie," I said softly. "It's Demary. I know you're feeling horrible, but can you tell us anything that will help us find the guy?" Her eyeballs swung toward me. Tears trickled down her bruised cheeks.

"H-hi, Demary." Her voice was a thin thread of sound. "I didn't see hi-hi-him t-till t-too late." I stroked her hand gently.

"But—but I th-think I—I know w-who..."

--- ★ ---

"Larkin has launched a terrific series here. She has a great premise and a knack for revealing bits and pieces of her characters as though she is trailing a fishing line."

—*Rendezvous*

HEAR ME DIE

E. L. LARKIN

WORLDWIDE.

TORONTO • NEW YORK • LONDON
AMSTERDAM • PARIS • SYDNEY • HAMBURG
STOCKHOLM • ATHENS • TOKYO • MILAN
MADRID • WARSAW • BUDAPEST • AUCKLAND

HEAR ME DIE

A Worldwide Mystery/September 2001

First published by Thomas Bouregy & Company, Inc.

ISBN 0-373-26397-X

Printed in U.S.A.

I would like to thank my friends and colleagues
in the Willapa Writer's Circle
for their encouragement and support,
and in particular Birdie Etchison,
Brenda Burnham and Judy Waughgal,
for their help and advice.

PROLOGUE

IT BEGAN ON Saturday.

The alarm buzzed at five minutes after seven.

Disciplined as ever, even at that hour of the morning, Sara Garland checked her watch and then shut her eyes for an extra ten minutes of sleep.

"Really, Sara, that is one of the silliest things you do," an amused male voice said. "Why don't you just set the blasted thing for seven-fifteen to start with?"

Sara's eyes popped open. She lived alone.

"And besides that, it's Saturday. What have you got the alarm on for anyway?"

Sara sat up with a jerk and looked around her bedroom. A total stranger gazed back at her from the chair beside the window.

He gave her a good-natured smile.

"H...h...how d—did you get in here?" Sara stuttered.

"With my key, of course. You didn't think I took our argument seriously, did you?" he asked, brilliant green eyes sparkling at her. He stood and walked over to the bed. "Up you get." He pulled her out of bed and into his arms.

Sara didn't resist. She knew she had never seen him before—no one could forget a hunk like this blond beachboy, but his calm assumption of a close relationship had her confused. His kiss, a light brush of his lips across hers, felt as familiar as a favorite daydream.

Recovering, Sara gave him a furious shove and lurched across the room. "Who the heck are you?" she gasped.

"Oh, come on now," he said, laughing. "You don't need to keep it up. I know you're sore at me, but not so mad you've forgotten me overnight, surely."

Sara didn't answer. Wide awake now, she stared up at him. Under her cap of Clairol-gilded hair Sara had a mind that worked with all the giddy abandon of an IBM computer. She wasn't frightened, reasoning that if the man had meant her any immediate harm he could have attacked or killed her as she slept. But neither was she really *not* frightened. There was no way of telling what he had in mind, and she was certainly no match for him physically.

She let her eyes fill with tears. They spilled

over and down her sleep-flushed cheeks. As she well knew, tears made her look like a Botticelli angel.

"Hey, sweetie, don't cry," he said quickly. "What's the matter?"

Sara despised being called sweetie. She nearly told him to stuff it, but managed to catch herself in time. "I don't remember you at all," she quavered in her best little-girl voice.

He laughed again. "C'mon, Sara, quit horsing around. We're due out at the Porters' place by ten and it's a good hour's drive from here, so hurry it up."

"Porters'?" The name did sound familiar.

"For brunch, silly. You told them we'd be there for brunch. Now get dressed and let's get going." He handed her the clothes, mirror, and makeup case stacked on the chest of drawers. "I'll get your swimsuit. Where are the beach towels? In the hall closet?"

Sara nodded dumbly. The beach towels were in the hall closet, and he had unerringly opened the right drawer of the dresser to get her swimsuit. She wondered if she was losing her mind.

She picked up the things waiting on the chest and retreated into the bathroom, wishing she didn't live on the fifth floor. Dressing hurriedly—there was no lock on the door—she tried to visualize the apartment complex in her mind. At the moment, her knowledge of the building looked like her only advantage.

He was waiting by the entrance to the outside hall when she returned dressed in a pair of blue cotton slacks, a navy T-shirt, and a multicolored madras jacket.

"Great," he said, holding out his hand. He had her carryall in the other. "You look great. We're running late though, so let's get with it."

"My purse. Where's my purse?"

"I stuck it in the bag here," he said, hurrying her through the front door.

The building's tiny elevator gave Sara a momentary twinge of panic. She didn't want to be shut into that small space with him.

The elevator stopped at the third floor to admit an older man and woman. As the couple stepped on and turned to face the front, Sara twisted her arm sharply, jerking away from the blond's loose grip. Before he could react she slipped through the closing doors and raced toward the fire exit she knew was around the corner of the hall. Behind her she heard the elevator start, stop, and start again.

She jerked the fire door open and let it slam

shut again with a resounding crash. With any luck the blond would think she had gone that way, and the noise covered what little sounds she made as she hurried through the unmarked door at the end of the hall that led to the mezzanine.

The mezzanine floor was empty and quiet. Sara stood in the shadow of one of the ornate support pillars and watched the main lobby below. The middle-aged couple from the elevator was just going out the front entrance. There was no sign of the blond man.

For a moment that worried her. She had no way of telling where he'd gone. She was sure he'd abandon whatever plan he had in mind now that she had gotten away from him, but she wasn't sure enough to leave the security of the lounge and go looking for the manager. He would have to let her back into her apartment. Her keys were in her purse. Fortunately she did have three quarters and a dime in the pocket of her jacket and there were telephones in the lounge at the back of the mezzanine.

The manager's phone was busy.

Sara thought for a minute, then called her boss at home. She was supposed to meet him at the company offices at nine-thirty and she was going to be late.

A man whose voice she didn't recognize answered the phone.

"This is Sara Garland," she said. "May I speak to Mr. Werner?"

"I'm sorry," he said after a moment's hesitation. "Uncle Carl is still asleep. May I take a message?"

Sara hung up without answering. The conversation, brief as it was, made her uneasy. She knew Carl Werner was an only child and that he had never married. Werner didn't have any nephews.

Irritated at herself—the man was probably only using "Uncle" as a courtesy title—she called the manager again. The line was still busy. Then, wanting contact with someone, she called a friend, Demary Jones.

ONE

I GOT HOME LATE Sunday evening after a long weekend sailing on Puget Sound. I'd gone with Jake Allenby and another couple Friday afternoon. We intended to come back the next day, but when we got to the approach to the Hiram M. Chittenden Locks—or as they are more commonly called, the Ballard Locks—on Saturday afternoon there was such a crush of boats waiting to go through Jake turned and tacked back out for a while. I got a wonderful shot of an outbound forty-footer with multicolored sails as we turned. I have a fantastic new camera that not only times and dates your snaps, it practically takes the pictures for you.

The lineup meant we'd have at least a four-hour wait before we could go through the locks to Salmon Bay where Jake ties up, so we finally decided to stay out another day.

Jake is a detective sergeant with the Seattle P.D., where wages certainly don't run to thirty-two-foot sailboats. However, he'd won a chunk of the Washington State Lottery a few months back and had spent every penny of it on an old secondhand boat. Sailing is a great sport and I'd had a wonderful time. Jake is always fun and so are the other two, Carol Ann Guginsberg, also Seattle P.D., and Frank Kettle.

It was a marvelous weekend but I was completely beat by the time we got back, too tired to do more than take a hot shower and fall into bed. I didn't even bother checking my answering machine.

I know it didn't make any difference when I got home or when I checked my machine, but I still can't shake the guilty feeling that if I'd returned on Saturday I might have altered the outcome somehow. Realistically I know better, but it doesn't change how I feel.

I didn't know that on Monday morning, however, and after listening to Sara's recorded voice for the second time, I called her number at the Electric Toy Company. Sara was ETC's head accountant.

Jean Cook, ETC's production coordinator, answered. I wondered what she was doing in Sara's office. Jean's little cubby of an office was at the other end of the building from Sara. She told me Sara hadn't come in yet. She was abrupt and sounded like she had a head cold. I started to tell her about Sara's call but she cut me off, saying she was busy and that she'd talk to me later. I had already tried Sara's apartment so I put the call on mental hold and got dressed to go to work.

My new Sag Harbor outfit in size eight fit perfectly. I'd been doing water aerobics and had lost nearly ten pounds. Unfortunately my sunburned nose didn't compliment the shirt's burnt-orange color. I'm not tall, not quite five foot two, so all my parts are close together. Short, naturally curly auburn hair, bright pink face, and pumpkin shirt just didn't cut it. I changed to an olive-green pullover and tan Dockers.

I own and operate a small investigative business, Confidential Research and Inquiry. With a degree in historical research, I work mostly in that field but I also do a lot of genealogy, some legal research, and a little P.I. work. My clients are mostly writers, although I do have a few law firms and insurance agencies as regular clients, too. It's cheaper for them to hire me. I have more experience so I'm faster at the work than their own people. One of my accounts, Harbor Insurance, sends me at least five names to trace every month.

My office is on Forty-fifth Street in the Wallingford district, just a few blocks from my house. Martha met me at the door, told me my nose was peeling, and handed me a cup of coffee.

"You've an appointment in an hour and two calls to make beforehand, Demary, so get in gear," she said. She bosses me around like a deckhand.

Martha Kingman is my associate, my secretary, my office manager, and/or anything else she feels like being. Black and beautiful, she is an even six foot tall with a figure like a board, Grecian features, and a caustic personality. Every now and then she tries to use her height advantage to intimidate me. It never works but she keeps trying. With her figure she can get away with wearing outrageously high-style clothes. Today she wore a tan linen sheath with a black patent belt and a row of shiny black buttons down the side. She looked fabulous.

"All three of these came in this morning?" I asked, obediently taking the memos she handed me. Three clients on a Monday morning was some kind of a record.

She nodded, naming two of my regular clients who were writers, and a third I'd not heard of before.

The calls were to the two regulars who had chronology projects they wanted me to work on. One was writing an epic romance and needed to be sure he had his dates and events in the right order. The other had a finished manuscript, a family saga, ready to send to his publisher, and needed the same thing done, yesterday if possible.

The personal appointment was something else entirely. His name was James Robert Dudley and he claimed to be a descendant of that sixteenth-century Dudley, the Earl of Leicester, who was the first Queen Elizabeth's ill-fated Master of Horse.

He didn't look the part. He was short, not more than five-seven, overweight by at least fifty pounds, bald as an egg, and had a lisp. His manner, however, was authoritative and crisp, and his story was intriguing.

After being introduced by Martha and shaking my hand he started out by asking how I pronounced my name. I was tempted to tell him Jones only had one pronunciation but on second thought admitted that my given name was pronounced De-mary, not Demry as my Scottish grandfather had pronounced it.

Dudley nodded, seeming to file the information away for possible future use, then got down to business.

Although he was a third-generation U.S. citizen, his family still owned property in England. On it a tenant farmer had recently unearthed a casket containing documents that appeared to have been written by the son of one of the early Plantagenet kings.

"I want you to go to England, Ms. Jones, and look them over with an eye to verifying their content," he said.

I thought for a moment. "I'm not sure that I can, Mr. Dudley," I said finally. "It sounds a little out of my line. I think what you need is a forensic scientist rather than a historian. And anyway, to start with, why don't you have the documents sent over here? Much easier to deal with if—"

"No, I don't want to bring them to the States," he interrupted. "There's too much red tape involved in taking any kind of artifacts out of the U.K. Before I get into all that I want to be sure I know what I've got. Once any government agency is involved I lose control.''

I could see his point, but I wasn't sure I liked the sound of it. He had gone a bit tense and I had a feeling that what he wanted of me was either illegal or dangerous, or both. Which wouldn't necessarily stop me; I don't mind bending the law now and then, but I like to be the one to make the decision.

''I'm still not sure I can help you,'' I said finally. ''I'm not an expert on the Plantagenets, and if I understand you correctly, what you are looking for is proof that a very young prince wrote the thing. Do you know if he could write? Many of those early—''

''That's exactly what I want you to do,'' he interrupted again. ''I'll get someone else to test the paper for age and all that. What I want you to do is find out if he could have written it at all. Find out if he could write and how well, where he was at the time the papers were supposedly drawn up, and if he had ever been in a position to meet the lady involved. Find out if it's possible he could have written it, not whether he actually did. I've been told you are good at that kind of thing.'' He gazed at me hopefully, adding, "And I want you to verify everything firsthand. At the source."

We discussed my fees, which I quoted high, and then I told him I'd get back to him later as I'd have to see if I could clear my calendar for such a trip. The last was pretentious nonsense to stall him for a couple of days. What I really wanted was time to research Dudley himself. Something about the man didn't quite fit the job he wanted done.

He wasn't happy about the delay; he seemed to expect me to leave on the next plane.

Martha was thoroughly disgusted when I told her to start checking him out—finances, possible police record, the whole nine yards. Martha is almost as good at that kind of thing as I am.

"What's the matter with you?" she demanded. "Maybe he is a wide boy. What do you care? As long as he pays up front it's a free vacation in England. Go!"

"And if it turns out to be dangerous and I get my head blown off?"

"Don't be silly. They don't do that kind of thing in England."

Although she was born in Barbados, Martha was raised in Liverpool, and despite ten years as a U.S. citizen she still speaks with a broad BBC accent, uses U.K. colloquialisms, and thinks more British than American.

"Read the papers. They do that kind of thing everywhere nowadays," I reminded her. "And anyway, I'm not sure I want to go to England. Why don't *you* go?"

She gave me a thoughtful look.

"In the meantime get me the Electric Toy Company, will you? I want to talk to Sara Garland." I went back to my office, straightened the citrus-colored wall hanging by the door, which Mr. Dudley had knocked askew, and started entering interview notes on him into my computer.

I had finished and was wondering why Martha was taking so long when she came to the door. A deep frown puckered her beautiful chocolate-brown face.

"Demary, Sara seems to have disappeared. In fact the police are looking for her."

"What?" A sharp frisson of fear raced up my spine. "Who told you that?"

"Jean Cook at Electric Toy. The whole place is in an uproar. Not only has Sara disappeared, Connie Black, their office manager, is in ICU. She was injured in a car accident Friday evening.''

''Connie? Oh, no.''

''And that's not the worst of it. Carl Werner is dead. Jean says he was murdered. Beaten to death!''

TWO

"WHA-AT?" MY MIND FROZE in neutral. I couldn't even think of a sensible question. Murder is always shocking, especially the murder of someone you know, but somehow being beaten to death seems particularly horrible.

I didn't know Carl Werner well but I had met and talked to him a number of times. I had known both Jean Cook and Connie Black for years. Jean lived next door to my parents.

Werner, who was sole owner of the Electric Toy Company, was, in my opinion, somewhat paranoid about security. I did a lot of employee reference validation for him. He insisted on having every single reference checked in detail and wanted it done in person if possible, which I thought a bit excessive. The company made electronic toys for children. He paid promptly, however, and I do like that.

Martha pointed at my phone. "I've got Jean on hold."

I picked up. "Jean, this is terrible. Why

didn't you tell me before? What happened, anyway?"

"I couldn't say anything before. The police have been here all morning and they wouldn't let me say anything to anyone. There were two of them in the office with me when you called."

"Are they still there?"

"Not with me but all over the place otherwise. Carl wasn't killed here, he was killed at home, so I don't know what they expect to find. Besides, you know what our security is like."

I did know. The devious security system Werner had invented not only covered the entire building, the offices were protected in addition by a very sophisticated electronic maze that included a silent alarm, video, and an intruder trap. It was highly unlikely that anyone could have circumvented the system. Carl Werner was an electronic genius.

"What happened? I mean, did someone break into the house or what?" I couldn't imagine how anyone could break into his house, either; it too was protected by his security gimmicks.

"They don't know yet. Or at any rate, they aren't saying. Apparently Borda found him yesterday morning when she went to see why he hadn't come down for breakfast.''

Borda Gruber was Werner's housekeeper.

''For heaven's sake, didn't she hear anything? She lives there, doesn't she?''

''Yes, but not in the main part of the house. She and her brother have the two bedrooms in the wing between the house and the garage.''

''What kind of questions are the police asking? Do they want alibis?'' I asked.

''No, not really. I don't think they know exactly when he died. But they are asking how we spent the weekend. I spent most of it at the hospital with Connie. Did Martha tell you about Connie?''

''Just that she was in an accident. Was she seriously injured?'' Connie Black was ETC's office manager. Between the two of them, Connie and Jean, they about ran the place. Both of them had been with ETC since Werner invented his first toy.

''Yes. Very bad. It was a hit-and-run.''

''Oh, no. What...?''

''She was starting home from Albertson's Friday evening when it happened. According to a woman who witnessed the accident, Connie was just leaving the parking lot when this pickup came roaring across several lanes, apparently trying to beat her to the exit, and skidded into her. He—it was a man driving—smashed in the driver's side door and then just peeled off and went tearing down the street."

"How awful. When did you hear about it?"

"The hospital called me. She was unconscious but she carries a card that lists me as the person to call in an emergency. I have one listing her. We made them out years ago when Bob died but we never thought we…" She stopped, choking back sobs.

"But she is going to be all right?" I tried to sound as if it was a sure thing.

"They don't know, Demary. She had her seat belt on but her head hit the door post. Her skull has what the doctor called a hairline fracture. They did some kind…" She stopped again, gulping back more sobs, then went on. "They did some kind of surgery late Saturday night to relieve the pressure on her brain but… but…they don't know yet." She began to cry in earnest.

I didn't know what to say. Not only were she and Connie close friends, Jean's husband, Bob, had been killed in a hit-and-run accident five years ago. The person responsible for Bob's death had never been identified.

I still wanted to speak to Sara, however, and after talking to Jean for a while longer I asked her to see if Sara had come in yet.

"She's not here, Demary, and I'm afraid something has happened to her, too."

"Oh, come on now, Jean. She probably had an errand to run or something. Tell her to call me when she has time. Okay?"

She said she would and hung up, still sniffling.

Martha had been listening on the other phone. She came back to the doorway now.

"What a dreadful thing. They must be devastated over there. But what's this about Sara? And why are you looking for her?"

Frowning, I took the tape from my home phone out of my purse and shoved it in the recorder on my desk. "Listen to this, Martha, and tell me what it sounds like to you."

Sara's recorded voice came on.

"Demary, this is Sara Garland. I'm... um...I'm on the mezzanine floor at my apartment house. When my alarm went off this morning a perfectly strange man was in my bedroom. He didn't hurt me; he pretended we

were...he pretended we were going to someone's house for breakfast. I got away from him
when the elevator stopped on three and an older
couple got on. They were there, so he couldn't
just tackle me. I ran down the hall and came
here to call Carl to let him know I'd be late
dropping off the TforToys disclosure he wanted
to see this morning, but a strange man answered. I thought I heard Borda in the background but...Demary, the man in my bedroom
is about six-two, a blond hunk with sun-
streaked hair, bright green eyes, and a California beachboy tan. He said—''

The tape clicked off at that point. There was
no way to tell from her voice if she had hung
up or if the time had run out, although I could
check the time.

"How bizarre," Martha said, frowning.
"You want to know what it sounds like to me?
It sounds like Sara is in a whole lot of trouble."

"It sounds the same way to me."

We stared at each other for a long minute. I
spoke first.

"I guess I'll call Sam."

Martha nodded. "I guess you darn well
better."

THREE

SAM MORGAN IS a lieutenant in the Seattle P.D. homicide division. Sam and I go back a long way, back to when I was a kid and still believed in flower power. He's a good-looking guy, kind of a combination Robert Redford/Paul Newman, but with dark hair and dimples.

We have a curious relationship. We almost got married once, but fortunately we came to our senses before we did anything so drastic. Sometimes we get along fine, sometimes we agree to disagree, and sometimes one or both of us are so mad at the other we don't even speak. At this point I guess you could say we are friendly antagonists. Sam has two really serious faults. He is ridiculously protective and he tries to tell me what to do, or what not to do, as the case may be.

True to form, he hates for me to have even the slightest connection with a homicide. He immediately turned shrewish when I told him about Sara's message and asked him why he was looking for her.

"Because she is very possibly involved in Carl Werner's death," he snapped. "And that tape could be an attempt to set her up with an alibi. Why would she have her alarm set on Saturday? The whole thing sounds like bull. However, I will send someone out to pick it up."

"That's stupid, Sam," I snapped right back, holding on to my temper. Sam has that effect on me. "I played it for you. How could it set up any kind of an alibi? I've known Sara for years. She would no more kill anyone than I would. And besides that, he was beaten to death. How could she—"

"Where did you hear that?" he interrupted. "There was a fight and he took a beating all right, but that wasn't what killed him. He certainly wasn't *beaten to death*. And I didn't say she killed him herself. She wouldn't be strong enough. Somebody gave him one heck of a chop."

"And you think Sara was part of that?" I demanded. "You're out of your mind."

"I don't know what her part was, but she was there. Her prints are all over the place."

"Of course they are." I was nearly yelling

now. "She was at his house all the time. My prints are probably all over the place, too."

"Why? Didn't he have an office? And what makes you think you know her so well, anyway? She's considerably younger than you are."

I swore to myself. Sometimes Sam could be seriously tacky.

"Well, you don't know anything about her at all," I said. "I do know her. I know most of the office staff at ETC, and besides that, Sara worked for Harry Madison for a couple of years when she first got her CPA license." Harry is my office neighbor. "We got to know each other then and have remained good friends."

"If you're such a good friend you'd better tell her to contact me and do—"

"Sam, didn't you listen to what she said?" I interrupted. "Someone tried to kidnap her. She got away but they undoubtedly found her again and who knows what has happened to her by this time. You've got to find her."

"We're trying."

I said something unprintable.

"Look, Demary, regardless of why, we are trying to find her. I put out an APB, we contacted her sister, Laura Hope, in San Francisco, and we're talking to her friends, the people at the toy company, and at the apartment. We *will* find her.''

Frustrated, I scowled at the wall, trying to think how I could make him take a more active interest in finding Sara. "What makes you think she had anything to do with Werner's death?" I asked finally. "And what did kill him if it wasn't the beating?"

For a bit I didn't think he was going to answer, then, in a more decent tone, he said, "There was a fight and he did take a beating. I think he may have gotten a few licks in, too. At some point, though, he fell; his head hit the side of a heavy chair and the fall broke his neck. Which may change the legal wording of the charge against the perps, but it's still murder.''

"What about Sara?"

He sighed. "We found one of her personal belongings near his body. And that's all I'm going to tell you, Demary, so don't bother asking. I'm sorry about it, but just because she's your friend doesn't automatically make her one of the good guys.''

"I didn't say it did, but finding something of hers in the house doesn't mean anything either.

Werner liked to work at home and he thought nothing of telling her or any of his other employees that he wanted to see them at home. Especially lately.''

''Why lately?''

''Because of the buy out, or merger, or whatever it was with TforToys last month. Both Sara and Anna Carmine, Werner's attorney, have been putting in a lot of overtime getting all the paperwork done.''

''Why at the house? Why not at the ETC office, or the lawyer's office?''

''I don't know why. But that was what he wanted, so that was what they did. He has a special shop in the basement where he designed and built the prototypes of the unique toys the company is famous for. He was very secretive about his toy designs and maybe he was working on something new. If so, he may not have wanted to go out to the plant everyday. Both Sara and Anna live in this end of town so it could have been more convenient for them, too.''

''What do you mean, 'special' shop? We saw his shop. What's special about it, other than some very expensive equipment? The housekeeper didn't point out anything unusual about it.''

"You probably just saw where he does some of the rough work. The place where he does his real work is hidden behind the shop you saw. He showed it to me a couple of weeks ago. Werner is...*was* a security freak as well as an electronic genius. The door to his special shop is masked by a trompe l'oeil painting of shelving that blends in with some actual shelving. That's where he keeps all his prototypes, too. He opened it with a gadget like a garage door opener that I think he had on his key chain. Did you find his key chain?''

"Yes, it was on the floor, but I don't remember...I'll have to look at it again. What were you doing at his house?''

I was getting tired of answering questions and not getting any information in return. I thought of telling him Carl and I were dating—that would irritate him to no end—but decided I'd better behave if I wanted him to keep talking to me, or to tell me anything later on.

"He hired me to run reference checks on the TforToys employees before he took over the business,'' I said, making a real effort to sound sweetly cooperative.

"Were they all okay?"

"All I researched was their references. They were fine."

"Knowing you, you checked more than that," he said sourly. "What else did you find out?"

"None of the people I checked had police records, if that is what you mean, but one was let go on a previous job because he was suspected of petty theft. I talked to his shift boss, who was positive the guy was stealing small electronic parts and selling them on the black market. He couldn't prove it, though, so no charges were ever filed. His name is Bert Elder."

"You're sure he doesn't have a record?"

"Not in this state, and as far as I was able to find out, he has always lived in or around Seattle."

"Did Werner keep him?"

"I believe so, yes. He would probably have let him go soon though. Carl was a fanatic about security and I told him the guy was high risk."

"Hmm. Jake or Ahern must have interviewed him. I don't remember the name. What's he look like?"

"I don't know. I don't think I ever saw him. He worked in the shipping department."

"We'll check him out. I've got to go...."

"Hey, wait a minute. I've got a couple of questions, too," I said quickly. "I thought this was supposed to be a two-way exchange."

"You thought wrong. Look, Demary, I've told you before, you're not a detective. Now get that answering machine tape ready for me to have picked up, and stay out of this."

He hung up.

I put my phone down with exaggerated care. This was what I got for being a good citizen? For, as the English say, helping the police with their inquiries?

I opened a drawer and took out a clean envelope, addressed it to Sam, dropped in a worn-out Tammy Wynette tape, sealed it, and took it out to Martha's desk to await pickup.

Nowhere did it say I had to play nice.

FOUR

IT WAS NEARLY one o'clock by the time I got over being mad. By that time I was hungry, so I called Jean at ETC and asked her if she wanted to meet me for lunch somewhere halfway between us. My treat. Werner's house is actually not far from my office but the ETC manufacturing complex is a ways north, out toward the Bothell area.

Jean said sure and named a Thai restaurant on Lake City Way near In the Beginning, a fabric shop that caters to quilters. Jean is a quilting fanatic. She won a blue ribbon at the Houston show last year with one of her children's quilts. She has no children of her own so she donates her quilts to the Children's Orthopedic Hospital for the little patients to take home with them.

I had forgotten today was the beginning of Seafair Week, Seattle's annual citywide whoop-de-do of parades, hydro races, ethnic performances, carnivals, dances, and pageants. The traffic was gruesome but even at that I got there before she did, and had just ordered a pot of chrysanthemum tea when she arrived.

She came marching over to me with her usual vigorous stride. Jean is about forty-five but seems younger despite her gray-streaked dark hair. She's ETC's production coordinator and although she doesn't look it she's as smart as a cage full of monkeys. She has a photographic memory when it comes to exactly what and how many of anything ETC has on hand.

She looked wretched, however, and nearly started crying again when I asked about Connie.

"I talked to one of the nurses in ICU just before I left the plant and they said there was no change yet. Demary, if I could get my hands on that guy I'd...I just don't know what I'll do without her."

Both she and Connie were widows and neither had any children. They had been friends for many years. It would be very tough for her if Connie didn't make it.

I'd always been curious about her relationship with Carl Werner, so to take her mind off Connie for a bit I asked why she hadn't liked him. They'd had a smooth working relationship but she had never made a secret of the way she felt about him.

She gave an unladylike snort. "Let me tell you, he may have been an electronic genius but he was no lovable old toy-maker by a long shot. He fancied himself a ladies' man and he had a mean streak a yard wide. It's a wonder some woman hasn't offed him before now."

"You don't think…"

"Sara had anything to do with his death? Good heavens, no. Not Sara, and anyway, he never bothered any of the women who worked for him. The toys were everything to him and he'd never have done anything to disrupt production. Which any kind of a harassment charge would certainly have done."

I must have looked surprised.

Her eyebrows rose. "You didn't know that about him?"

"No, never even got a hint. He sure never came on to me."

"Some P.I. you are. Actually, he was no dummy—he'd know better than to try anything with you."

"What does that mean?"

"What? Oh, smart enough not to come on to you?" She smiled. "Well, let's just say you have a certain something about you and it isn't

French chic. You'd have chopped him off at the knees and he knew it."

Come to think of it, I would have. Men who think signing your paycheck gives them patting privileges raise my rudeness factor by ten.

The little waitress brought our order just then and we both dug in. I'd ordered one of their specialties that has shreds of chicken and vegetables mixed with rice. It's spicy and sweet at the same time. Wonderful!

After a while Jean went on. "The police came to the house and got me this morning so that they could get in the plant without setting off the alarms. They went ahead of me into every room at the place so I can't be sure, but I don't think any of the security was breached. They think it was but I didn't see any evidence of a break-in. Certainly not in the assembly line, or the storerooms. Nor the office. The safe was closed but not locked, but then it seldom was."

"No one broke into it?"

"No. Nothing much of any importance is ever kept in it anyway, except maybe the cover designs for some of the packaging. It's left open half the time."

"How about the toy patents and blueprints and electronic stuff?"

She shook her head. "No, nothing valuable is kept in it. In fact I think the only reason he bought it was because it's decorative."

"Decorative?"

"Mmm, yes. It's an antique, huge with lots of fancy brass scrollwork on it and a hand-painted picture of a train on the front. I don't know how easy it is to open, but I do know anything of any consequence is in the bank vault or in his head."

"In his head? You're kidding."

"No, really. When he was working on a new toy it was all in his head, all the electronics especially. I think he did most of his calculations on a blackboard and immediately erased them. You know how secretive he was. In fact, I don't think he ever put anything on paper until he built the prototype and tested it."

"How do you test a toy?" I asked, and then realized how. "He gave it to a kid to play with, yes?"

"Sure. How else?"

We had finished eating and were working on a fresh pot of tea when she said, "I've been so worried about Connie I haven't thought much about Carl, but I do wonder who could have done it. Borda, maybe—his housekeeper."

"Sam said Carl took quite a beating. I can't see any woman being capable of that. Besides, Werner was no lightweight. He'd fight back, and Sam will be looking at everyone for evidence of being in a fight. Anyway, what would be her motive? Seems to me someone told me she had worked for him for years."

"Yes, she has, but I think that's mostly because of her brother, Millard. A horse kicked him in the head when he was a toddler and although he's nice enough, mentally he's still pretty much of a child. I don't know but I'm guessing that was part of the agreement when Borda came to work for Werner. Letting Millard live there, I mean."

"How old is he?"

Jean shrugged. "I don't know, thirty maybe."

"Could he have done it?"

"I doubt it. I don't think he has the mental capacity and he's too timid. He's big and strong and does all the heavy work around the house that Borda tells him to do, but like any kid he doesn't do a very good job unless she keeps an eye on him. He ends up playing in the water when he's supposed to be washing the windows. And anyway, from the few times I've seen him I got the impression Millard was afraid of Carl.''

"What makes you think Borda might have killed him?''

"I don't, not really. I was just talking, but she did have a good motive. I've been in the house a lot. Carl had that shop in the basement where he always made his prototypes and he was forever telling me to bring him some part or another from the factory. And from what I saw he was a bugbear to work for at home. Not like at the plant.''

"What kind of person is she? The only time I've ever seen her was when she answered the door.''

"She's nice enough, I guess,'' Jean said, shrugging. "She was pretty in a buxom, Germanic kind of way when she first came to work for Carl, but she isn't anymore. She's only thirty-five or so but she looks a whole lot older.''

I frowned, trying to remember her more clearly. The only picture I could call up was of a rather heavy-bodied woman with gray-blond hair pulled back in a severe bun.

Jean checked her watch and got up. "The doctor said I could call him at two-thirty and it's almost that now. I'll be back in a minute. I'll use the phone at the desk.''

Watching her sturdy little figure go off toward the front, I was struck by an unpleasant thought. One of Werner's specialties was a maze. He started the toy company with an electronic maze game and the office security was built on a very sophisticated electronic maze principle. Only four people knew how to circumvent it. Werner, Jean, Connie, and Sara.

Was Jean the only one left?

FIVE

LATER, DRIVING BACK DOWN I-5 to the office, I had some awkward thoughts about the Electric Toy Company's security.

If the office had been prowled as the police seemed to believe, prowled as opposed to being broken into, it had to be an inside job, but by whom? Jean had an ironclad alibi. She had been at the hospital the entire time from seven-thirty Friday evening to four o'clock Sunday afternoon. As had Connie.

Or did they have an alibi, either one? Did anyone know when the supposed intruder had been there, or for sure that there had even been an intrusion? Sara could have left the place unsecured accidentally. Also, although I didn't believe it, Jean or Connie or any combination of the three of them could have ransacked the place before they left Friday afternoon. On the other hand, maybe the security system had never been turned on. Who was responsible for arming it? That was something I needed to find out.

If the police had no idea when, or even if anyone had actually been inside the building, nor for sure when Carl Werner died, Carl himself could have left it open any time between Friday evening and whenever he was killed.

It was even possible that the two things had nothing to do with each other. I had to admit that would be stretching coincidence to the breaking point, but stranger things had happened.

At the moment, then, anyone of the four people who knew the system could have unlocked the doors and even the safe. Jean said that several of the new men who had come to ETC with the TforToys merger were electronic wizards. One of them might have figured out the system. One, Allen Johnson, had been the top man at TforToys.

So where did that leave me?

Hey, hold on, I told myself sharply as I turned off I-5. *Who hired you to investigate anything? Just because you're ticked off at Sam for telling you to stay out of it doesn't mean you have to do a one-eighty and jump in with both feet. You have four* paying *jobs you're supposed to be working on. Looking for Sara is one thing; sticking your nose into Werner's death is unprofitable. Dumb, too.*

Tires screeching, I pulled into my parking space behind the office and went inside. One of the other tenants, Harry Madison, who is a CPA, was sitting on the end of Martha's desk talking to her about our landlord.

Our former landlord had died a year ago and left our building to his grandson, Ira Sharin, who was doing his best to make us all move. He wanted to tear the place down and build a multistoried business and apartment complex. Unfortunately for him we all had at least four years to go on our leases and did not want to change locations.

Another tenant, Anna Carmine, is an attorney and she assures us Sharin cannot force us out, but Harry isn't all that certain and he's determined to keep his office where it is. Harry is a permanent-press kind of guy who likes everything cut and dried and hates any kind of change. He'd been trying to get me to investigate Sharin with a view to finding some dirt we could use to pressure him into leaving us alone. To me that smacked of blackmail, so I'd been stalling.

He started in on me again as soon as I came in.

"Demary, I'm not asking you to frame the man," he said, scowling at me. "All we need is something that will keep him off our backs. Maybe he's cheating on his wife. That would work."

Martha snickered.

"Are you serious?" I asked, wondering if he had ever actually met Sharin. "Have you ever taken a good look at him? He apparently doesn't believe in bathing and has the physique of a slab of bacon and the personality of a mud slide. I'm surprised he ever found a woman willing to marry him, let alone go out with him."

"Well, there must be something you can find out. Just follow him around for a while; you know the kind of thing. You're bound to find out something he doesn't want known."

"I doubt it. He strikes me as a very careful guy. And anyway, I've told you before, that isn't what I do. You're an accountant—maybe he cheats on his taxes."

"And how am I supposed to find that out?" he demanded angrily. Muttering to himself, he gave up and went stomping off toward his office.

"I swear, I think he's going around the bend," Martha said, rolling her eyes. "He's been telling everyone he's got you on Sharin's trail and that you're sure to find something murky enough to save the day."

"He'll get me sued for harassment, is what he'll do," I said crossly.

Still looking amused, Martha handed me several message slips and told me I had a call to answer also. One message, from Sam, I crumpled into a ball without bothering to read. One was from Anna Carmine, our resident lawyer, asking if Martha could do some extra work for her.

Four other businesses share the building with me. We share the front reception area where Martha works and to some extent we share Martha. She is receptionist for all of us. I'm her primary employer, however, so they always ask when they want her to do something extra. They pay her extra also, which is fine with me, as I couldn't afford to pay her what she's worth on my own.

"You may have been right to be skeptical of

Dudley," she said now. "His phone number is disconnected."

I frowned at her. "Why in the world would he give us a phony phone number?"

"I didn't say phony. It's disconnected." She stopped, staring into space for a moment before she went on. "Now that I think about it, he didn't want to give me his number, said he'd call us. He finally did give it to me, though, probably figuring that we wouldn't bother calling him. And normally he'd be right."

"Doesn't make sense. It isn't as if he'd given me a check or anything." I thought a minute. "Well, no harm done. We'll see what happens."

I worked for a while on a genealogy project I was doing for a woman in Wyoming. She was a fun client. She got my name in the most roundabout way you could imagine. I had done some work for a local family who recommended me to a woman living in Florida. The woman in Florida moved to South America, started a correspondence via the Internet with a teacher in New Mexico who corresponded, again via e-mail, with my Wyoming client. I loved it. Computers are wonderful.

Martha stuck her head in the office at four-thirty and said she was leaving, so I packed it in, too. I wanted to get out to the Blue Owl before five anyway.

The Blue Owl is a small neighborhood tavern a block or so from the Electric Toy Company that specializes in a wonderful variety of sandwiches made with their own homemade bread. The owners are a middle-aged couple who do not allow smoking, swearing, or any kind of rough behavior. They sell more soda pop than they ever do beer. A bunch of ETC employees stop there after work nearly everyday. With any luck Werner's murder would be the number-one topic of conversation tonight and I just might learn something useful.

I didn't want anyone to know I had any particular interest in Werner's murder, however, so I was careful to join a group that included Judy McDonald. She had been to England the year before and I used talking to her about Dudley as an excuse for sitting with them. Actually, my only real interest in Werner's death was its possible connection to Sara's disappearance, so I didn't need to be so cautious. Plus, there was so much talk about Werner's death and the possible break-in going on around the whole room, nobody paid any attention to me anyway.

Everyone at the table, five besides myself, knew about the security system and none believed anyone could get past it. The general opinion seemed to be that if the safe had been looted it had been left ajar Friday evening. They all seemed to think the safe held both money and important papers.

I wanted to know what they thought, or knew, about Sara's disappearance, but it took me a while to work the conversation around to her. When I did I got a surprise.

I sensed rather than saw a ripple of interest at the table next to us where three men were sitting. I couldn't tell who but I knew somebody at that table was listening to our conversation, listening hard. He, or they, had definitely reacted to Sara's name.

SIX

"WHAT MAKES YOU SAY Sara is missing?" Judy asked. "I mean, maybe she just took the week off for Seafair. I would if I could afford it."

"Mmm. Maybe," I agreed, trying to figure who was listening so hard. I hadn't intended to tell them about the message tape, anyway, but I certainly wouldn't now.

One of the women at our table asked if any of us knew Borda. "I heard one of the cops say the whole room where they found Werner was torn up and there was blood all over the place," she said. "Seems funny Borda or her brother never heard anything. Although I did hear once that the brother was kinda simpleminded, so maybe he wouldn't pay any attention."

She turned to the next table. "Allen, you been out to Werner's house, you think it's so big she wouldn't hear anything?"

"Huh?" The man with his back to me turned. "What did you say?"

"I asked if you thought Werner's house was

so big the housekeeper couldn't hear what was going on.''

He shrugged. "I've never been inside. It looks plenty big from the outside, though."

When he'd turned I recognized him. Allen Johnson, who had come to ETC with the TforToys merger. He was a good-looking guy, about six foot with sun-bleached blond hair and a great physique. And a black eye with accompanying cut on his cheekbone.

My heart went into a double-time routine. I was so surprised my mouth went into gear before my brain had time to engage. "Where did you get that?" I gasped, nodding at his face. I can really be stupid sometimes. If he'd even been near Werner's place he sure wasn't going to tell me.

One of the other men at his table guffawed.

"Sorry, none of my business," I said hurriedly.

The woman across from me giggled. "Go on, tell her, Allen," she urged.

Allen swore. "You'd think I was the only one who ever walked into a door," he snapped. "Some idiot opened his car door just as I was going between the two cars and I walked into it. That's all there was to it."

"I'll bet," the giggler said archly. "Who was she, Allen?"

He started to answer, obviously irritated, but changed his mind and laughed good-naturedly. "Betty, you know what? You're a pain, that's what. Ask Bert, he was with me."

Bert, at the next table, admitted he was there and verified Allen's story. "It was Allen who was the idiot, though," Bert said, grinning. "There he was, blood pouring down his face, ready to clobber whoever had opened the door, when out gets this gal who looks like a sumo wrestler and before old Allen here can open his mouth she starts bawling him out for not looking where he's going."

Everyone else at the table had apparently heard the story before, because they were all laughing. Allen looked as if he wouldn't mind clobbering Bert at this point, but Bert went right on.

"So guess what our hero did," Bert chortled. "He apologized!"

Everybody howled with laughter, me included. Which didn't necessarily mean the story was true.

After the merriment died down Allen shifted his chair so he was facing our table and started talking to the man beside me about the electronics of one of ETC's latest toys. As I understood very little of what they were saying I tuned them out and tried again to isolate whoever it was that had been eavesdropping.

Several rounds of beer later, I was still working on my first glass of wine. Allen turned his attention to me and after some preliminary small talk asked, "I'm getting hungry. How about taking in a steak with me over at the Keg?"

"Can't," I said regretfully. Any other time I would have said sure, but I was too worried about Sara to enjoy anything tonight, even dinner with a gorgeous hunk like him. His eyes glimmered with the promise of all kinds of fun and games. "Can't manage it," I repeated. "Rain check?"

"Sure." He gave me a wide, white-toothed smile. "Same time tomorrow?" He made a hand circle at the crowded tavern.

"I'll try." I bid the table a general adieu and took off for home hoping I didn't get stopped by a cop. I had only finished half my glass of wine but I don't normally drive with even that little aboard.

It had been pretty much of a wasted evening

as far as learning anything significant, but I had gotten an overall feeling for the group. Almost all of those at the tavern worked the production side of ETC, and Werner's assembly line being what it was, they were unlikely to know much that pertained to the office or engineering side.

Werner's security mania included the assembly line. He had set it up in such a fashion that it was impossible for those working the line to know what was being made from the parts they produced. The many miniature pieces they put together were made in small quantities on a rotating basis and stored in locked bins in a locked storage area until needed on the finishing tables.

In fact, now that I thought about it, I wondered how the man next to me at the table had been so knowledgeable about the toy he and Allen Johnson had been talking about. Something to do with a spy game and overhearing private conversations. Allen had been a designer for TforToys but I didn't think he'd done anything like that for ETC. In fact, I was pretty sure I remembered hearing that he was looking for another job.

I gave my house an appreciative once-over as I pulled into the drive. I own a super place.

My great-aunt left it to me in her will. It looks like a Victorian wedding cake with acres of gingerbread trim, diamond-shaped shingles, and leaded windows. Tall and narrow, it is only forty-five feet wide including the wraparound porches on all three floors. All the rooms have ten-foot ceilings with ornate plastered corners and hardwood plank floors. I have three bedrooms, five fireplaces, and a kitchen the size of a skating rink. It does have a couple of disadvantages. No garage—it fell down before my great-aunt died—there is only one bathroom, and for some weird reason the kitchen and dining room are on the second floor.

The house was in run-down condition when I got it but I've gradually had things upgraded. One of my first additions was a top-of-the-line security system including automatic outside lighting—Sam badgered me into that—and last summer I had the whole place painted. My intention was to add another bathroom this spring but after hearing what plumbers charged per hour, I raised my own rates and decided one bathroom was all anyone needed anyway.

Someone called my name as I got out of the Toyota.

"Hey, Demary, wait up."

My teenage pal, Joey Winters, came pelting down the sidewalk. Joey is thirteen, thin, wiry, and tall for his age. He adopted me a couple of years ago.

He came to a stop in front of me and gave me a big smile, showing off his new braces. I was glad he'd told me in advance he was getting them or I might have said something unsuitable. His mouth seemed to be full, and I do mean full, of huge metal nuts, bolts, square bits, and wires. As it was, the first thing I said was bad enough.

"Joey, don't they hurt?" I asked. There was a thin crust of dried blood at the corner of his mouth.

"Naw, not anymore," he assured me. "My mom got the sicks, though. I told the doc to make her stay home next time. She don't need that kind of aggro. She's got a wimpy gut."

Joey speaks a language all his own.

I deduced his mother had been somewhat upset by her first sight of his mouth, and very possibly by the blood spots on his T-shirt. Although she may not have noticed them. The shirt featured a monster of some sort being stabbed to death by a willowy female in a scanty fur bikini. I've often wondered if his mother needed glasses.

"I'm sorry about your friend, Mrs. Black," he said. "I saw it happen. Is she going to be okay?"

"You saw Connie get hit?" I exclaimed. "Did you talk to the police?"

"Naw. No point. I was clear over on the other side of the lot helping my mom load the groceries in the car. I wasn't looking that way. Turned around fast enough when I heard the crash but didn't see much. I might recognize the truck if I saw it again but I didn't get the number or anything. Didn't see the guy driving at all."

"If you see it, the truck, you tell me right away. Fast, okay?"

"Sure. You on the Werner case?" Joey asked, his eyes sparkling with interest.

"The Werner case? How in the... How did you hear about Werner?" I demanded. "And what makes you think I'd be interested in Werner, anyway?" Joey is the kind of kid who not only knows everybody in the neighborhood, he knows every *going on* in the neighborhood, but Werner's place was a little far afield. The house was several blocks away and there had not been anything in the paper yet.

"Oh, I have my ways," he intoned archly.

"Joey!" My voice rose.

He grinned. "The doc lives in the same block as Werner and his girl has the hots for me."

"That is not the way to talk about a little girl," I said sternly, wondering what TV show he'd heard that expression on. I thought it had gone out of style. "Who are you talking about, anyway? Werner doesn't have a daughter." I was really at sea.

Joey sighed. "Doc Casey's kid. The orthodontist. She and Millard were hiding in the bushes. They looked through the window and watched the cops. Saw them bag up the body and everything. She told me all about it."

"Good grief! How old is she?"

"Six. Maybe seven."

I got a grip on myself. "Well, what made you think I might be…whatever. I'm not on a case of any kind, Joey, so forget it." Joey had elected himself my deputy sometime ago and he is hard to dissuade. He's a natural-born snoop.

"And tell your little girlfriend to stay out of the bushes," I added. "Not only will the police take a dim view of them spying, whoever murdered Carl Werner is no one to fool around with and he just might get the idea they do that sort of thing all the time.''

''They do,'' Joey said cheerfully.

SEVEN

"DO YOU THINK I should call Dr. or Mrs. Casey?" I asked Martha the next morning.

"What did you tell Joey?"

"I told him to warn Deana away from Werner's house entirely. At least for the present. But I don't know how much good him telling her will do."

"At her age she might be more apt to listen to Joey than she would to her parents," Martha said, frowning a little. "Joey said they made a practice of peeping? How old is the boy? Willard?"

I explained about Millard.

"Sounds like a rum setup. I hope you told Joey to stay away from the place, too."

"I told him all right, but you know how he is when he takes a notion to play detective. And he did hear something kind of interesting. He said lately Borda has been locking Millard in his room on weekend nights. He has his own bathroom and a television, so it isn't as if he's miserable there but he says it makes him mad, and I wonder why she does it.''

Martha got up and went over to look at the coffeemaker. It was making gurgling noises. ''He told Joey that?'' she asked, unplugging the machine.

''No, he told the little girl, Deana, and Deana told Joey. Joey says he's never been able to talk much to Millard, although he's been over there several times in the last couple of weeks. Since he started at the orthodontist, I guess. He says Millard is scared of his own shadow and doesn't talk to anyone unless he has to.''

''Maybe he walks in his sleep or something.''

''Apparently she has never done it before. Have you emptied the trash this morning?''

''Have I what?''

''Emptied out the trash basket. What was in that memo from Sam yesterday?''

She shook her head. ''If I remember correctly it was something about your playing stupid games, and to get that tape down to him immediately.''

''I thought that might be it. I think I'll run a copy and take it down to him right now. I'll tell him I picked up the wrong tape by accident.''

Martha gave an unladylike snort.

SURPRISINGLY, SAM DIDN'T SAY a word when I handed him the cassette. I didn't bother with an excuse. We both knew why I'd done it.

While he was using the phone to call someone to come get the thing, I craned my neck to see the top photograph on a stack in front of him. It was a shot of the front room of Werner's house.

''Take a look,'' he said, elbowing the stack toward me as he put the phone down.

Which should have warned me.

The second print in the bunch was a picture of Werner's body, in full glowing color.

To say it was frightful was a gross understatement. For a moment I thought I was going to lose my breakfast. His face was so battered I would never have recognized him if I hadn't known who it was supposed to be.

''Take a good look, Demary,'' Sam said acidly. ''And maybe you'll see why I want you to stay out of this.''

''You think Sara...'' I swallowed hard. ''You think Sara had something to do...''

''I told you before, her prints are all over the place,'' he said in an uncompromising tone.

"And I told you why. If prints are all you've got, you're so far out in left field you aren't even in the same county, Sam. My prints are all over the place, too."

"We found them."

"Then what the heck is your problem?"

He sighed, obviously deciding whether or not to even answer me. "All right, Demary. Her pocket appointment book was under Werner's body."

I stared at him, trying to assess what finding it meant. "Just lying there?" I asked finally.

"Well, Werner wasn't clutching it, if that's what you're asking. It was simply under him."

I took another, closer look at the photograph of Werner's body. It was half on its side, lying close up against a big chair. His head rested under the edge of a small end table.

"And that proves she was there when he was killed? Don't be ridiculous. The D.A. would laugh you out of his office and you know it," I said, suddenly furious at him. "She could have left the thing anytime. Probably right there on that table. It doesn't prove a thing."

He shrugged, refusing to give an inch.

Trying to control my temper, I walked over and stood looking out the window at the plaza in front of a public building across the way. A magnolia in full pink-and-white bloom marked the center of the little square. I couldn't remember what the building housed.

If it wasn't simply an accident, if leaving Sara's date book under Werner's body was a deliberate attempt to incriminate her, where did the killer get it, and was that the only such attempt made?

"Is that the sole thing of Sara's you found?" I asked, turning around.

"Besides her fingerprints? Yes." He leaned back in his chair. "What does that tell you?"

"It tells me the date book isn't worth diddly as evidence of any kind," I said, exasperated. Sometimes Sam can be so impossible to pry information out of he makes a clam seem garrulous. "Sara isn't an idiot. If she was involved in his murder she'd know better than to leave anything personal around."

He just looked at me.

"Sam, be sensible," I pleaded, changing my tune. "Sara's fingerprints don't mean a bit more than mine do. What about the woman who lives there? Borda? What does she have to say?"

He picked up a pencil and started doodling on some papers in front of him. "All right, Demary, she says the same as you do, that Sara was there frequently, but that isn't the reason I'm interested in her whereabouts. Everyone agrees that only four people were familiar with the security system and Sara is one of them. At the moment that's my main interest in her."

I decided to try another tack. "Do you know yet when he was killed?"

"The M.E. says sometime between midnight and six Saturday morning. He'll get it a little closer when the pathology is done. We know it couldn't have been before one because he didn't leave his lady friend's place until a little after twelve-thirty. Actually, he should be able to pinpoint the time pretty close from the stomach contents. The lady says they had a bowl of popcorn about eleven while they were watching the late movie on TV."

"Where was Borda all that time?"

"Asleep from around ten that night until eight in the morning, when she got herself and her brother up. She left early Saturday morning to take her brother to the parade and didn't get back until seven that evening. She claims Werner had told her she could have Saturday off, didn't need to fix him any breakfast, and could leave as early as she wanted."

"And she never heard anything the night before?"

"She says not. She doesn't sleep in the house. She and the brother have a three-room suite, including a small kitchen, in a wing between the house and the garage, so she didn't go into the main part of the house at all until Sunday morning."

"So, no alibi."

"No motive either. Sara does have."

The phone rang and I decided to leave before we got into another squabble. What possible motive could Sara have?

Carol Ann Guginsberg was standing by the elevator when I reached it.

"I told you to use more sunscreen," she greeted me. "Your nose looks like a peeled strawberry."

"Well, thanks a lot, you look great, too," I retorted as we got aboard the elevator.

She grinned. "What happened to your sunny disposition? You been talking to Sam?"

"If I strangle him one of these days will you swear I was talking to you at the time?"

"I think he found out you spent the weekend on Jake's boat."

"It's none of his business what I do. On the weekend or any other time."

"Well, I'll bet it'll be a hot day in December before Jake gets another three-day weekend off." Laughing, Carol Ann got out on second and trotted away around the corner of the hall.

I fumed the rest of the way down to the main floor. It was sometime later before it dawned on me that in his ham-handed way, Sam was, as usual, simply trying to keep me out of harm's way.

Right then, as luck would have it, when I got to the outside door I spotted Jake Allenby across the way in the plaza.

"Hey, Jake, wait for me," I called, racing across the intersection. Jake greeted me with a bear hug.

I hoped Sam was watching out the window.

"What are you doing here, Demary?" he asked, steering me toward the entrance to the underground garage. "How about having lunch with me?"

"Sounds good."

"I'm on my way up to Providence Hospital to see if I can talk to Connie Black. They said she is more or less conscious. We can eat in the cafeteria there. They have better food than half the restaurants around.''

''How come you're going to see Connie? Do you think the two things are connected? Werner's murder and the hit-and-run?''

He shrugged. ''No, but until we talk to her we can't be sure. The timing is suspicious but in itself it looks more like coincidence. The two witnesses both say the truck skidded into her, nothing deliberate about it. Also both say the driver was a kid and if so he probably panicked.''

''So he ran.''

''That's what it looks like.''

''Anything on the truck? Year, make, color, whatever?''

''Not much; it happened too fast. Several people thought it was blue but for some reason Connie's car didn't have any paint traces on it from the truck, so we don't know what color blue. One witness said skyblue, whatever that is supposed to be; another said turquoise, so it's anybody's guess. The truck got away so quickly no one had a real look at it.''

''Maybe Connie saw more.''

''Let's hope so, otherwise we're up that famous creek without a paddle.''

CONNIE'S DOCTOR was in the hall when we got to the intensive care unit. He said Connie was coming along fine.

"She is recovering far more quickly than I expected," he said after Jake had produced his ID. "She's conscious most of the time and so far, doesn't show any signs of brain damage. Really remarkable."

"May I talk to her?" Jake asked.

"You can try. She's still not entirely lucid but it won't hurt to make the attempt."

He gave us a cheery smile and waved us through the swinging doors.

I tagged along behind Jake, trying to look as if I belonged. Which may not have been strictly ethical, but it wasn't my fault if both the doctor and nurse thought I was a cop. Jake didn't care.

Connie was conscious, but only just. Her eyes were open a bare slit. All of her that wasn't swathed in bandages or covered by the sheet was streaked dark maroon and black. IV tubes fed things into both of her arms and she was in some kind of a padded brace that kept her from turning her head.

"She knows you, doesn't she?" Jake whispered, sounding as appalled as I felt. "Do you think she'd recognize you?"

I nodded. I didn't trust my voice.

"Try."

I moved to the side of her bed where she could see me. "Connie," I said softly. "It's Demary. I know you're feeling horrible but can you tell us anything that will help us find the guy?"

Her eyeballs swung toward me. Tears trickled down her bruised cheeks.

"H-hi, Demary." Her voice was a thin thread of sound. "I didn't see hi-hi-him t-till t-too late."

I stroked her hand gently.

"B-but I t-think I-I know who... T-tell J-Jean, too..."

The lines on the monitor above her head were flickering wildly and a second later a starched nurse literally jerked us away from the bed and out of the curtained cubicle.

"Out," she hissed. "Get out of here. She's too weak for this. Get out."

We got.

EIGHT

WHEN I WENT BACK to work Anna Carmine, my office neighbor, was talking to Martha. Anna's rooms are at the far side of the building and although I know her reasonably well as a co-tenant, we aren't acquainted beyond that. About fifty years old, tall and angular, with dark brown eyes, a wide mouth, and black hair cut in a Liza Minnelli style, she is a striking-looking woman without being at all pretty. She has a sharp reputation as a trial lawyer. I know if I was an attorney I wouldn't care to have her as an opponent. She has the courtroom de-meanor of a thwarted bullterrier and I'd heard she could be positively lethal with an uncertain witness.

"Good afternoon, Demary," she said, hold-ing out her hand. "I've been waiting to talk to you. Do you have some free time?"

"Sure, come on in," I said, leading the way into my office. I hoped she didn't want to dis-cuss our landlord. I was getting tired of hearing about him.

I smiled to myself as she turned one of the tangerine-colored leather chairs to face my desk and sat down. A tan chair sat right beside it but the tangerine one was a more dramatic contrast to the lime-green outfit she was wearing. In or out of the courtroom, Anna was never unconscious of her image.

"I know you and Sara Garland are friends," she said without preamble. "Do you know her sister?"

I shook my head. "Not really. I know about her but I've never met her. She lives in San Francisco. Her name is Laura. Laura Hope."

"Yes. She called me last night and will be up here late this afternoon. I don't know why, because I've never done any work for her, but Sara has apparently given her my name as the attorney to contact in case of an emergency and she wants to retain me to sue the police department for slander, defamation of character, libel, unwarranted scurrilous remarks, and character assassination. Oh, and I think dereliction of duty. Her words, not mine."

"Good grief!"

"Yes. Well, I think I convinced her that filing such a lawsuit wasn't in her best interest, but I'm not sure what else she might have in mind. From the sound of it, maybe boiling Lt. Sam Morgan in oil.''

''I might give her some help with that. What in the world did he say to her?''

She grinned. ''Nothing really. Certainly nothing actionable. That is, he wasn't explicit, but according to her he insinuated that Sara was guilty of a number of unspecified crimes. Do you know anything about her, Demary? Is she as flaky as she sounds?''

''I don't think so. But Sara did say she has a temper. She's a real estate broker. Owns her own agency. Her husband—I think his name is David—is a publicist. He specializes in organizing marathons.''

She raised her eyebrows. ''He does what? Organizes marathons?''

I nodded. ''Right. Sounds a bit unusual, I admit, but apparently it's quite profitable. Or at least so Sara said. He's also a CPA. She never said anything against him but from her tone of voice I don't think she cared much for him.''

''Strange way of making a living. I wonder what he's like personally.''

''I have no idea. I've never met him. I think Sara said he, or actually both of them, are fitness nuts, work out in a gym three or four times a week. He's some kind of a karate expert, too.''

"Hmm. Well, at any rate, what I'm here for is to ask if you will take her on. Laura, I mean. I'm not in a position to accept her as a client. My status is too ambiguous. You do have a P.I. license, don't you?'' she asked sharply.

"Yes, I just renewed it,'' I admitted. The only reason I'd done so was to bug Sam, but I didn't tell her that. Sam doesn't like me having a license, even though I had one long before I met him.

One of the first jobs I had after graduating from college was for George Crane, who owned C.R.I., Confidential Research and Inquiry. At that time it was a private eye place. I started out as a general assistant but he insisted I get a license. I turned out to be good at some of the work. Snooping comes natural to me, too.

After George was killed in a senseless drive-by shooting I stayed on, more or less inheriting the place by default. George had no known relatives and his only assets were some beat-up old furniture, so I put my name on the door and tried to remember everything he'd taught me. One of the things he'd told me was to beware of lawyers.

So I asked this one why she didn't want Sara's sister as a client.

"It isn't that I don't want her," she said. "I'm too involved with ETC and Carl Werner, which makes working for her a possible conflict of interest. I can't be seen to be working for anyone suspected of being involved in his death even if that someone is as far removed as Laura. Plus, there is another facet. As far as I can ascertain—"

I held up my hand. "Hold it a minute. Let me play something for you." I told her about the tape and played her my copy. "For my money Sara is a victim, not a suspect," I said when it clicked off. "And furthermore there is nothing I know of that involves her in Werner's death." I disregarded the date book. As I'd told Sam, Sara could have left it in Werner's house anytime in the past.

Anna sat for a moment, her face blank and still as she thought something out. "Do you have a dollar?" she asked abruptly, holding out her hand.

"Is that old ploy actually valid?" I asked, digging a bill out of my purse and handing it to her.

She nodded. "You have now retained me, so

anything we say to each other is privileged information. And as you are not in anyway involved in Carl Werner's death I can suggest to Laura Hope that she hire you to clear her sister's name."

"Why did I hire you?" I asked.

She nodded at the tape. "You are of the opinion that Sara is not only innocent of any wrongdoing, you think it possible she has been kidnapped and you need legal advice as to how to go about proving your points." She grinned. "Sounds good, anyway."

(Consulted later, Martha's opinion was that it was the biggest load of codswallop she had ever heard.)

"How can representing Sara's sister be a conflict?" I asked, going back to the original point. I couldn't follow her reasoning. There wasn't any connection between Laura Hope and Werner.

She ran her fingers through her hair, leaving it standing up in points all over her head. "This whole thing is so convoluted, I... To back up a bit, I drew up Werner's will and I'm also one of the executors. Sara is one of the beneficiaries. If Sara is involved in the murder, she can't inherit, but if not, and if she's dead, her sister

Laura will inherit one third of ETC. Provided she was alive when Werner died. Werner left ETC to Sara, Connie Black, and Jean Cook.''

That was a surprise. Although, maybe not. I knew he had no kin, so why not those three? Which didn't answer my question.

"I still can't see the connection," I said.

"You haven't heard it all. I researched this last night. I didn't draw up Sara's will, actually didn't know if she had one, but I explained the problem and asked her sister if she knew. She told me they had made out identical wills years ago, each leaving their estate to the survivor. So, if Sara doesn't reappear, and/or isn't cleared of complicity, Werner's estate will be tied up in the courts for years. And he left a huge estate. Plus there is a time element but we'll ignore that for the moment."

"You've lost me somewhere along the line, but never mind explaining, I'll take your word for it."

Anna got up and paced back and forth across the room. "In brief, it's vital for everyone concerned that Sara be found. And more important, be proved innocent of any wrongdoing," she said.

"I think it's a bit vital for Sara, too," I said, somewhat tartly.

She stopped her pacing and swung around to face me. "I'm sorry, Demary. That did sound pretty cold, didn't it? I didn't mean it that way. It's simply that I'm in such a—"

"How did you know she was missing?" I interrupted.

"A detective from Seattle P.D. called me. Regarding Werner, of course. The housekeeper, Borda, had told them I was his attorney. He also asked me if I was in contact with Sara. Sara and I aren't close friends by any means but I've known her for sometime and know disappearing like this isn't like her. I was concerned as soon as I heard she hadn't come to work, but now, after hearing your tape, I'm really worried. Unfortunately, the position I'm in ties my hands as far as doing anything personally."

I didn't agree with her but I'm no lawyer so I didn't argue. I was looking for Sara anyway so if her sister wanted to pay me for doing it that was fine with me. If Werner's murder happened to be involved, so much the better.

And if Sam didn't like it, too bad.

NINE

AFTER ANNA LEFT, Martha came in with the mail. "Take a look at this," she said, handing me a check.

It was a personal check drawn on the account of James Robert Dudley, for twenty-five hundred dollars. The memo line in the bottom left corner bore the word *Retainer* in small, precise script.

"Well, what do you know," I said thoughtfully. "Do you suppose it's any good?"

"It is. I called the bank to make sure. He uses the same bank we do."

"Was there a note or anything with it?"

She shook her head. "Nothing. I checked the phone again, too. It's still disconnected and it is Dudley's number. I verified that while I was at it."

"Have you had time to find out anything else about him?"

"Very little. He doesn't own a car, nor have a driver's license, at least not in this state, and neither does he have a police record of any kind."

"I wonder if he could be using a phony name?"

"Possibly, but both his bank account and telephone are in the name he gave us."

"I suppose the phone could be some kind of a mix-up. On his part, I mean. He could have been out of town, forgotten to pay his bill, whatever."

She shrugged. "Maybe, but not likely. The phone company doesn't disconnect unless you're way, way behind. Or have had problems with payment before. I'll check property taxes, trade unions, and professional organizations this afternoon."

"Mmm. Well, don't take this to the bank, stick it in the safe. We'll see what happens." I handed the check back to her. I try never to cash a retainer until I'm sure I want the writer for a client. Much easier to say no if you can hand the check itself back. Which always irks Martha. She thinks money belongs in a bank earning interest.

She went back out front and I turned to my computer to open a file on Sara. I didn't have much to keyboard in other than a verbatim tran-

script of her phone message and what little
Anna had told me. There just didn't seem to be
any hard information that had a bearing on her
disappearance. At the moment I was disregard-
ing any connection to Werner's death. I did not
believe she could be involved.

One thing I had overlooked, though, were her
friends, what few of them I knew. Anyone of
them might know something about where she
had gone. If *gone* was the correct word. I still
felt she had been taken somewhere rather than
gone anywhere willingly.

I didn't know who she was currently dating,
and besides, he would surely be working at this
hour, as would most of her women friends. But
there was one person who would not only be
home, she knew me, or at least we had met and
she would recognize my name. Mrs. Ireland.
Mrs. Ireland was an elderly widow who had an
apartment in the same building as Sara. The two
of them had met several years ago and had
struck up a conversation over Mrs. Ireland's
dog. A conversation that had been the start of
a friendship.

Actually, Mrs. Ireland's dog had bitten Sara
on the ankle, but that had not kept them from
liking each other. Mrs. Ireland and Sara, that is.

Sara never did care much for the dog, a shih tzu with the personality of an irritated chipmunk.

The lady was at home and quite willing to talk to me when I explained why I was calling.

"I can't imagine where she could have gone," she said. "I was a little surprised when I didn't see her in church on Sunday but I thought perhaps she had gone to an early service. She does sometimes when she intends to go out to that new place of hers later. If she fell or hurt herself somehow she could be just lying there in the bushes and nobody—"

"What place?" I interrupted. "Where? What bushes?"

"Oh dear, I forgot. She doesn't want anybody knowing about it until all the papers are signed and it really is hers. She says it's bad luck to talk about—"

"Mrs. Ireland. What place? Where? Is it somewhere in the mountains?"

"Oh, good heavens, no. It's in Skyway. She took me out there a week or so ago to show it to me. I haven't seen her since. It's a lovely little house on a sort of back road with all kinds of trees and shrubs around it. A gardener's delight. Very overgrown at the moment, but—"

"Do you have the address or do you think you could you find the place if I took you out there?" I asked, interrupting again.

"Of course I could," she said tartly. "Just because I'm seventy doesn't mean I'm senile, you know, but I'm not sure Sara would want me to. As I said, she was superstitious about anyone knowing she was buying the place until it was a done deal. Although from what she said I think her offer was accepted and she was just waiting for the final papers. But still..."

It took me a few minutes to overcome Mrs. Ireland's scruples but in the end I drove over to the apartment and picked her up. I made both her and Tsu-tsu, the shih tzu, comfortable in the passenger's seat and we headed for Skyway.

The traffic was simply horrendous. Movement through the International District was almost at a standstill because of the Bon Odori festival. It was nearly six o'clock before I made the turn off Rainier Avenue.

Skyway is a district, rather than an independent township, that lies between Seattle proper and Renton. The whole area is hilly and some of the streets seem to have been designed with goats in mind rather than cars. Not only did they wander along the hillsides in ever-

changing directions, a number of them ended in
unmarked blind alleys. I had to retrace my way
several times but eventually we arrived in front
of a neat little bungalow surrounded by a huge
yard that was indeed overgrown. The long-
untended lawn was knee-high, while the shrubs,
hydrangeas, azaleas, lilac, forsythia, and a
dozen others I couldn't name spilled out of the
weed-filled beds. A real estate sign with a sold
banner tacked diagonally across the front of it
leaned against the porch railing.

There were no near neighbors and despite its
unkempt look the house had a lovely setting. I
checked the neighborhood automatically as I
rang the doorbell and then peered through the
window alongside the porch. What I could see
of the room inside was totally empty.

Mrs. Ireland trotted around the yard looking
under and through the shrubbery. For her age
she was a lively little thing. Dressed in a sensible brown print dress and low-heeled brown
shoes, she reminded me of a sparrow chirping
busily away at its own affairs. She had left Tsu-
tsu in the car where he was protesting shrilly.

Wishing I'd worn something a little more
suitable than my yellow linen dress and white
sandals, I made my way around the house push-

ing my way behind the greenery to peer through all the windows. None of the rooms held anything but dust and cobwebs.

I was struggling to extricate myself from a particularly clinging vine when Mrs. Ireland joined me, carrying a picnic basket.

"You know, I don't believe Sara has been back since we were here ten days ago."

"What makes you think so?" I asked, tweaking leaves out of my hair.

"This picnic basket. We left it by mistake and it was still there under the trees at the end of the garden. There's a tiny little creek down there. We sat on the bank and ate our sandwiches that day. If she had been back she would have put it in the car."

I frowned. "Maybe she just didn't want it anymore."

"No. You see, it's mine, and she felt quite bad that we had forgotten to pick it up. She wanted to go back but we were already halfway home so I insisted we go on. I know she wouldn't have left it a second time."

We made our way around to the front of the house and down the walk toward the car, where Tsu-tsu was still carrying on like a maniac. The dog didn't actually bark, he screamed.

"Why don't you let him out?" I asked. "He can't hurt anything."

"He'll run away. He's a stupid dog, doesn't have any sense at all," she said in an acerbic tone. "My husband loved him, though, so I can't bring myself to get rid of him."

I had to laugh. She sounded so provoked. I couldn't tell whether it was with herself, her deceased husband, or the dog.

Finding the house didn't seem to have much bearing on Sara's disappearance, but thinking it over I realized it at least answered the question of why Sara had her alarm set on Saturday morning. She meant to go out there and wanted an early start.

"Mrs. Ireland, I didn't think to ask you before but did you by any chance see Sara on Saturday?" I asked as we got back into the car.

"No. No, as I said, I haven't seen her since she brought me out here, a week ago last Sunday. Why do you ask?"

I told her about Sara's phone message.

"That sounds most ominous," she said. "Have you located the couple who got on the elevator?"

"I haven't but I'm hoping the police are making an effort to find them."

"Hmm. I haven't heard of them making inquires. I'll have to ask. Sara said the man was a total stranger?"

"Yes."

"Very strange. How would a stranger know she was alone?"

I smiled to myself. That was a tactful way of putting it. Mrs. Ireland wasn't unaware of what went on in the world today.

Which led me back to thinking about the guy she was currently dating. If he wasn't the man in her bedroom that morning, how had the guy gotten in? She had only mentioned this new man to me once and then only in an aside. We were talking about something else entirely. I couldn't remember what, however, nor could I remember his name but something she'd said about him was floating around the back of my mind, nagging at me. He was someone she had only recently met, I remembered that, and I had a faint recollection of her saying I knew him, but when and where escaped me.

Who was he, and why hadn't he contacted someone about Sara being missing?

TEN

I WENT TO MY AEROBICS CLASS the next morning and didn't call Sam to tell him about Sara's house until a few minutes after noon. Actually, I waited until I thought he'd be out of his office. I didn't want to talk to him. I was still ticked off at his thinking Sara had any part in Werner's death.

But he was in, and his first words were an apology. Then he told me the bad news.

Sara was dead. Her body had been found in the trunk of a stolen car.

"Oh, no," I whispered. "No! What happened?"

He didn't want to tell me. He hemmed and hawed around but finally said, "She, uh, she was strangled. Manually. The M.E. thinks probably late Saturday morning. He won't know for sure until after the autopsy."

"I told you, I told you!" I yelled, starting to cry.

"I know," he said gently. "But it's not your fault, Demary, so don't take off on one of your guilt trips. It happened long before you heard her message.''

"How did you find her? And where?" I demanded, tears streaming down my face.

"Two kids found her body earlier this morning.''

"Kids?"

"Two six-year-olds. Fortunately I don't think they understood what they saw. We offered to send one of the staff psychologists out to counsel them but the parents didn't think it would be necessary.''

"Did you talk to them? The kids?"

"Not much. It was strange. Neither one of them seemed to realize that she was real, and I didn't push it.''

"How horrible. Maybe they were in shock.''

"No. That's what got to me. They were both so matter-of-fact. Both families live across the alley from this empty house. It's for sale and has been for nearly a year. It has a big backyard and the kids like to play over there. While they were there this morning their two dogs got into the garage. They said they knew the garage door was open a little but they had never gone inside before, and probably wouldn't have gone this time if the dogs hadn't been barking so much. It's dark inside. Anyway, when they went to investigate they found the dogs jumping at the trunk of this car. The sleeve of a madras jacket was caught under the latch and the dogs were trying to tear it loose. The boys pushed the trunk open saw what was inside and ran home.''

''And it didn't frighten them?''

''Apparently not. They went back to one of the mothers and calmly told her that they had found a dead woman. She said they were both excited but so unconcerned she thought they were making up a story. According to her, the boy's exact first words were, 'Mom, come look. We found a dead lady, and she smells rotten!'''

I shook my head, feeling sick. Television had a lot to answer for. Children become so inured to scenes of death and violence they think it's a normal way of life. But maybe it was better that way, for these children at least.

Sam went on to tell me more particulars, which surprised me. I can never predict what he will or will not tell me. In this case I would as soon not have heard the details. A body that has been shut inside a closed car trunk for more than four days in eighty-degree weather doesn't make for appetizing details.

"Do the people at ETC know yet?" I asked.

"Yes. Ahern is out there talking to them now."

After we hung up I wiped my face, no doubt wiping all my makeup off along with my tears, and went to tell Martha. She was as distressed as I was; she knew Sara well also. We spent some time trying to console each other but there is really no way to rationalize such a brutal crime.

It was a while before either of us went back to work. I turned on my computer and brought up my file on Sara, keyboarding in everything I knew, as opposed to those things I believed to be true, and sat studying what I had. After a while I started a subfile listing the things I was sure were correct regardless of whether I had any proof of them or not. When I ran out of anything more to add and read it through I was provoked with myself to realize that almost everything I'd entered concerned Sara and Sara alone.

Apparently my subconscious didn't really care who had offed Carl unless, of course, he, they, or she was also responsible for Sara's death. A stupid perspective, to say the least. It was certainly possible that the two crimes weren't connected but it was highly unlikely. I needed to look at the whole picture if I was going to find Sara's killer, and find him, them, or her I would.

I gave myself a little more time, then called Jean out at ETC. She answered in a numb, dead voice that mirrored how I felt.

We didn't talk long. There just wasn't anything to say. She did tell me Connie was continuing to show improvement and they thought they would be able to move her out of ICU very soon. That at least was good news.

Later, I had gone back to work on the second file, when Anna Carmine called me. Sara's sister, Laura, was in her office, would like to meet with me, and could they come over?

"Does she know about Sara?" I asked, very softly. If Laura didn't already know I didn't want her to learn by overhearing me tell Anna.

"Yes, we know." Anna cut me short.

Laura Hope was the older of the two sisters. According to Sara she was a typical yuppie, drove a BMW, worked out three times a week in an expensive health club wearing name-brand sweats, maintained a year-round tan, and wore hand-tailored suits she ordered from Italy.

She did not have any children and did not want any.

She was also beautiful, or would have been if she hadn't looked so stressed. She had straight blond hair cut in a fashionably ragged style and turquoise-blue eyes with long dark lashes.

She shook hands with a firm, brief grip, told me Sara had spoken of me often, and seated herself in one of the tangerine-colored chairs.

She accepted my condolences gracefully but her primary emotion seemed to be rage. She didn't waste anytime on pleasantries. When she spoke her voice shook with suppressed anger.

"That detective, Lt. Sam Morgan, called me this morning. He told me about Sara's death and then he had the unmitigated gall to say it was her own fault," she said. "I will never forgive him for that and I intend to see him suffer for his insinuations. He said—"

"Hold it a second," I interrupted. "Let's get—"

"Demary, you have to understand—" Anna spoke at the same time.

Laura ignored both of us and kept right on going. "He said Sara was a member of a gang and that her death was a falling out among thieves. He said she—"

"Hold it!" I yelled this time. "Just hold it," I repeated when she stopped in midword, looking startled. She apparently wasn't used to being interrupted. "First things first. Why are you here? In my office, I mean. What do you want from me?"

"What do I want?" She shot Anna a surprised look, then swung back to me. "Why, I want you to find Sara's killer, of course, and make that filthy man eat his words."

"To start with, Ms. Hope, you need to understand that although I have a private investigator's license, that is not my primary business," I said with some formality. I wasn't sure I liked this lady and wasn't about to get chummy with her. "I do quite a bit of genealogy, some skip tracing and some validation, but most of my work is in research of one kind or another. Plus, I wouldn't have any kind of official standing."

Which had never stopped me before, but I didn't tell her that.

"Yes. Yes, I understand," she said briskly. "Sara told me all about you and Anna has already gone over that. And she told me about the telephone message you got. But she still recommended that I hire you. Will you do it? Find Sara's killer and make that revolting man—''

"Don't continue bad-mouthing Sam unless you can substantiate your complaints," I snapped, losing patience. "Heaven knows I can get furious at him myself, but I can't believe he actually said Sara was a member of a gang. What he more probably said was that Sara was one of only four people who knew the security system and that made her a possible suspect in another murder." I couldn't believe I was actually defending Sam but I went right ahead doing it.

"He said as much to me," I went on. "And it did make me mad, but I have sense enough to know that is the way he has to think. That's his job. He didn't know Sara, and the circumstances do point to her as a possible."

Anna stared at me, her eyes wide with surprise. She started to say something but before she could get the words out we were both unnerved by a rising wail of misery as Laura's stiff posture and controlled facade crumpled to the floor. Literally.

Laura had slid off her chair and was hunched up on the floor with her head on her knees, crying hysterically.

ELEVEN

IT TOOK SOME TIME and all three of us—Martha had come racing in when she heard the commotion—before we had Laura calmed down enough to talk again. At one point I thought I was going to have to go get Dr. Birdwell from next door. Eventually, however, her sobs subsided and she let us help her back into her chair.

"I'm sorry," she whispered through a belated hiccup. "I just can't believe she's gone. She was all I had."

I wondered how her husband would view that sentiment.

Anna patted her on the back while Martha, ever practical, handed her a paper cup half full of the medicinal brandy she kept in her desk. Laura gulped down the fiery spirits without seeming to notice what she was drinking. In a minute or so some color came back into her face and she again apologized.

"Forget it," I said, going back around my desk to sit down. "You've had a bad time to say the least. You're entitled to a few tears.

Where are you staying? Would you like one of us to run you back there?"

"No, I'll be all right. I'll take a cab." She wiped her face with a tissue. "I don't want to go back there now, anyway. I'm staying in Sara's apartment, or I was. I don't know how long..." She turned to Anna. "I forgot to tell you. This morning, when that man called me, he said he wanted to search Sara's apartment. I told—"

"He what?" Anna, who had been leaning against my printer stand, straightened with a jerk. "He has no right to search her apartment without a warrant. What did you tell him?"

"That is what I told him. He said he had one."

"That no-good..." Anna swore.

I scowled at her. Their attitudes were beginning to get on my nerves. I didn't agree with Sam's thinking in regard to Sara but I could certainly understand it and so should Anna. As things stood he had to consider Sara as a possible suspect in Werner's murder. Plus, and I knew he'd have this in mind, searching the apartment could well substantiate Sara's innocence rather than her guilt. If the lab boys could find traces of her Saturday morning visitor it would go a long way toward validating her taped message.

Which I told the both of them in no uncertain terms.

"Let's just agree that while Sam may not be your favorite lawman right now he does know the law. He knows what he has to do and what he can and cannot do. He couldn't get a judge to sign a warrant without due cause, as you well know, Anna, and if the lab guys do their normal job you'll hardly be able to tell they were there. When did he tell you they'd be through?"

She took a shaky breath. "He didn't say."

I picked up the phone and dialed Sara's number. It rang ten times before I hung up. "There doesn't seem to be anyone there now, so I'm sure you can go back anytime you want. Did you check the place out when you arrived?"

"What do you mean?"

"Did you look around to see what, if anything, could be missing? It might be a good idea if you took an inventory."

"I don't think I'd know if anything was missing or not. I mean, I haven't been up here for nearly a year and I don't really remember what she has...had." She swallowed hard, tears in her eyes again.

The arrogant veneer Laura had arrived with was sadly askew. In fact, she looked so miserable I surprised myself by repeating my offer to take her home.

This time she accepted.

By the time we got to the apartment Laura had recovered her composure and I realized she wasn't the virago I'd taken her for. It was painfully apparent that she was distressed, but she had herself well under control.

"Will you come up?" she asked. "I'll make coffee. I need a cup myself."

I thought maybe she also needed company for a bit so I agreed. "Yes, I'd like to look around, too. I've been in the apartment a number of times. In fact, I was here just a couple of weeks ago. I might spot something that the lab boys missed."

I wasn't too hopeful but I did go over the place as well as I could without disturbing anything while she made coffee. It didn't take me long; it was a small apartment. One bedroom, one bathroom, a kitchen with a small dining area, and the living room. I didn't find anything significant.

Laura put a coffee carafe and two mugs on a tray and brought it into the living room where

Sara had two chairs and a low table placed in front of the window. The window framed a spectacular view of Lake Washington and the Cascade Mountains, which even at this time of year were capped with glistening snow.

We sat without speaking, enjoying the scenery for several minutes, before I got to thinking about something I had done as a teenager.

"Laura, when you and Sara were kids did you have a special hiding place?" I asked.

"No, not that I remember, anyway. We were raised in a small house. There just weren't any hideaways."

"I don't mean that kind of hiding place. I mean where you hid your treasures, or something you didn't want the other one to see. Or..."

Laura leaped off her chair with a whoop, nearly scaring me out of my wits.

"Of course," she said eagerly. "The bathroom. In the bathroom." She raced across the room with me right behind her.

"Be careful," I warned as we crowded through the bathroom door. "Show me where but don't touch until I get my camera." I don't know why I was so sure we'd find something, but I was, and we did.

Adhesive-taped to the underside of a shelf in the towel cupboard was a hand mirror. I took a half-dozen pictures of the thing in place and then pried it off using a couple of tissues to cover my hands. I laid it, glass side up, in the middle of the bed. On the clear surface, written with an eyeliner pencil, dated and timed, was a note from Sara.

The man who made these fingerprints was in my bedroom when I woke up.

Four fingerprints, just above the note, were circled with eyeliner pencil.

"This proves Sara was telling the truth," Laura said excitedly, turning to the bedside phone. "I'm going to call that man."

"Wait," I said, holding the receiver down. "Let me think for a minute. This doesn't actually prove anything. Not as it stands. We need more."

"What!"

"Now don't get all bent out of shape again, but think about it. If, as Sam is forced to at least consider, Sara was involved in Carl Werner's murder, both the telephone message and these prints could easily be an attempt to establish an alibi. I don't believe it, but it would be possible."

Frowning, she stared at me for a minute before she asked, "What do you suggest?"

"First let me get some pictures of these prints, then tell me how you knew she hid things that way."

For a second I thought she was going to start crying again but she answered in a tight, controlled voice.

"Sara and I have always been very close, even though there are four years between us. Our parents were into their forties when I was born, forty-five and -six I think, and almost fifty when Sara came along, so that by the time I was sixteen our mother was sixty-one. I know all teenagers think their parents are totally out of it, but Mother really was a bit behind the times. She would not let me even wear pink lip gloss until I was in high school and at that point Sara, of course, was not allowed any makeup at all."

I smiled. "So you let her wear yours."

She nodded, her lips curving into a smile as she remembered. "Both of us bought makeup with our allowance, too. And that was how we hid it. We had an old wooden cigar box taped to the underside of a shelf in our bathroom.

Mother rarely came in there, anyway, but we always kept it hidden.''

The strained lines around her eyes softened. ''Sara was such a funny little thing. I don't know what I'm ever going to do without her.''

''Sara said you were raised in Albuquerque. What made you settle so far apart? With Sara in Seattle and you in San Francisco, you didn't have much chance to be together.''

''We didn't intend it that way, it just happened. David received a wonderful job offer in San Francisco, so of course that was where we went. Sara followed several years later, but she wasn't really happy living with us, so she came here to go to school. But despite the distance Sara and I remained close. We both wrote at least once a week, sometimes twice, and we talked to each other at least once a week also.''

''What in the world did you find to write about that often?''

''I told Sara all about my clients and David's. She told me about her friends—you were one— the men in her life, and of course the toy company. That's how I know about the money in the safe.''

''Money? What money?'' I asked, feeling a surge of excitement. This was the first I'd heard about any money. In fact, if I remembered correctly, Jean said the only money ever in the office was what was in the petty-cash drawer.

"What money?" I asked again.

"The money Carl put in the safe. The money that whoever broke into the place must have been after. Sara said it was one heck of a lot of money to be just lying in a tinny little safe. She didn't say how much it was, but she said it was a thick stack of bills with a rubber band around them. The other time he left the money in the safe like that it was in an envelope."

So many questions flooded my mind I couldn't think which one to ask first. This could change the whole complexion of the two crimes.

TWELVE

"I STILL DON'T UNDERSTAND why you don't want to tell what's-his-name, Lt. Morgan, about the mirror," Laura complained as we went back into the front room. I'd persuaded her to have another cup of coffee while I sorted out what I wanted to do.

"Oh, we'll tell him," I assured her, plopping back into my chair. She wandered around the room, absently picking things up and setting them down again without looking at what she was doing.

"First I'd like to have some hard facts to hit him with," I told her. "I want to make darn sure he takes the prints seriously enough to run them through the F.B.I. for a make. Immediately."

"Huh? I don't understand. Why wouldn't he?"

"If he gets stuck on the idea that they're a plant he'll waste time looking for a match on the local level. It could take several days, sometimes even a week or more to get an answer from the feds. Depends on how busy they are. So he might, as I say, try for a local match first, which could waste time." She still didn't look as if she understood but I dropped the subject and instead asked the question that was uppermost in my mind. When had Sara told her about the money Carl Werner had left in the safe?

"Friday night."

"Sara told you, or wrote?"

"She told me. She called to tell me she had signed the papers on the house that morning and while we were talking she said Carl had left this bundle—that was her word, bundle— of money in the safe that afternoon."

"You knew about the house already?"

Laura gave me a puzzled look. "Of course. I'm a real estate broker. Sara wouldn't buy a house without my vetting the purchase agreement. And anyway, it wasn't a secret."

"It was, kinda." I told her about Mrs. Ireland.

She laughed. It was the first time I had heard her sound even at ease, let alone actually amused about anything. She had an attractive laugh. It changed her whole face.

"Sara was so silly, so darn superstitious. She

was afraid if she really counted on anything it wouldn't happen.''

Tears filled Laura's eyes and she turned away to look out the window. Suddenly I wanted to cry, too. Sara had counted on the house and now she would never see it again. I knew Laura was thinking the same thing.

After a while I went back to the money. ''Did she tell you anything else about the cash?''

''Not really. She said Carl came into the office about four-thirty, tossed the bundle into the safe, and told her to be sure she locked the thing before she went home. She was annoyed at him because she said the safe was worthless, a three-minute job. Which, I think, means a safe-cracker could open it in less than three minutes.''

I nodded absently, wondering where Werner had acquired a ''bundle'' of greenbacks at that time of day, and why he hadn't deposited it in the bank.

''Did he tell her where he got it? She would have to enter it in the books. Did he tell her how to credit it?''

''She never got a chance to ask him. She said he wasn't in the room thirty seconds. He came in, tossed the roll into the safe, and left.''

"And she didn't have any idea how much it was?"

Laura rubbed her forehead with her knuckles, her eyes scrunched up in concentration. "I...I don't know. I can't remember. So much has happened I...I'm sorry."

"That's okay. Take it easy. If she told you, it will come back to you. No one else has mentioned money at all. I don't think Sam knows about it. It's a prime motive for both crimes and we'll tell him so."

"Will he believe me?"

"Yes, I think so. Or at least he'll believe that is what Sara told you. And I think he'll keep an open mind about it despite maybe still considering Sara a suspect. The thing is, the safe was shut but not locked when the police got there Monday morning and there was no real indication of a break-in."

Laura scowled.

"Was he in the habit of leaving large sums around so negligently? Did Sara ever say?"

"Just that one other time as far as I know. He was careless with money, though. Or so Sara said. She said he didn't seem to care about money."

"He must have made plenty."

"And then some. Those toys of his weren't dollar-ninety-eight specials. They were pricey. Any toy idea that is a hit is worth millions. I can't even begin to guess how many millions board games such as Monopoly have made for their owners."

"I wonder what Carl did with it. He lived rather simply for that kind of income. Did Sara know about his will?" If she knew, it was going to be another mark against her. No wonder Sam felt she had a prime motive.

Laura nodded her head yes. "He told her some time ago. She didn't like the idea but wasn't too worried about it because it was a death-do-us-part deal."

"Huh?"

"She would only inherit if she was working for him at the time of his death and she knew she wouldn't be. She had every intention of starting her own business as soon as she had enough money saved. I would have financed her anytime even if David didn't like the idea, but she didn't want that."

"Your husband? Why was he opposed?"

"He wasn't really opposed, he just didn't think she had the expertise to run a full-service accounting business. He's a CPA also. He was wrong, but it doesn't matter now.''

"One third of ETC will be yours now.''

She shuddered. "I can't imagine anything I want less. Anna told me how he left things, and as far as I'm concerned those other two women can have the whole shebang with my blessing.''

I asked her if she knew anything about Sara's current boyfriend.

"There wasn't anyone special. She had a couple of dates with someone from that other toy company but it wasn't anything important.''

"From TforToys? Someone who came to the Electric Toy Company with the deal? Or just someone who worked at TforToys?''

"I...I'm not sure. I think he came to work at Electric Toy. She said he was a real hunk but it wasn't a big deal. Just a couple of casual things. They went out to dinner after work once and once he took her to see the Mariners at the new dome.''

"What's his name?''

"I'm not sure. It was something simple, John maybe, but I...I'll ask David tonight when he calls, he might remember. I might have mentioned the guy to him.''

"Did she talk to him also when she called you at home?"

"Very seldom."

"Well, do ask him, please. See if he remembers anything about a new boyfriend. We know from Sara's message that the man in her bedroom was a stranger, but I'd still like to talk to anyone she dated. Did you bring her letters with you?"

She shook her head, her face bleak. "I've never kept them and now...now I'll never get another one." She groped in her purse for a tissue, managing to pull out everything else in the process. I picked up her makeup bag and a small leather case holding a picture of a good-looking guy with blue eyes, kinky-curly blond hair, and a wide smile.

"This your husband?" I asked, handing it to her.

"Yes, that's David." She stuffed bag and picture back in her purse.

"Good-looking."

"He thinks so," she said, shrugging.

I didn't comment. She sounded as if she was having marital problems and I didn't want to hear about them. I got up and walked over to the other window. It looked out over the courtyard and parking area where a woman with a small boy was unloading bags of groceries. There were several older couples in the courtyard either strolling or sitting on the concrete benches placed under the trees. Any one of them could be the couple who were in the elevator on Saturday morning when Sara was kidnapped. I wondered if Sam had made any effort to find them. If not, maybe I would get Joey to ask around. He got on well with older people. He liked them.

Laura and I talked for a while longer but didn't come up with anything, and I was about ready to call it a day when Laura let out another of her whoops of excitement.

"What? What?" I demanded.

"I just remembered. Sara did count the money. Ten thousand dollars. She told me she entered it into the computer under miscellaneous income. It will be there in the bookkeeping system. That will prove she's innocent."

"I don't know about that, but it will go a long way toward showing that she didn't have a motive. She could have just pocketed the money; no one else knew about it."

I picked up the phone and started dialing. I

could hardly wait. Sam was just going to love our turning up all this.

In a pig's eye he would.

THIRTEEN

I SPENT THE NEXT half hour in a delightfully acrimonious conversation with Sam. I suppose I should be ashamed of myself for hassling him. Sam's problem isn't that he resents my finding something that he's missed, he just hates my having anything at all to do with a homicide. He has always been ridiculously protective. After all, I'm not a ten-year-old, but ever since I'd nearly gotten myself killed investigating another murder he'd been obsessive about it.

It wasn't his fault the lab boys hadn't found the mirror, either, but I was still ticked off at him for suspecting Sara, so I didn't tell him about the money. Laura jumped on me about that the moment I hung up the phone. She wanted to know why not.

"Because I want to make sure it's in ETC's records before I say anything," I told her. "I'm not giving him anything else to hang on Sara just in case she meant to enter it but for some reason didn't."

"She said she had entered it."

"We'll make sure first."

"How are you going to do that?" Laura asked, looking dubious. "You can't just walk in and start snooping through a company's financial records. It's probably illegal."

"I'll think of something," I assured her. Actually I didn't have to think about it but I wasn't certain I wanted to share my methods with her. I didn't know her well enough.

I'd simply have Martha use the modem and access their main frame from our new Pentium. Jean wouldn't care and I doubted if there was anyone else at ETC with the expertise to detect Martha's presence in the system. And Anna would probably okay it anyway. The only problem was how secure ETC's system might be. With both Sara and Carl gone, getting into the bookkeeping files could be a problem if they were programmed with some of Carl's intricate security barriers, but if anyone could access them Martha could. She's a computer genius. She *thinks* like a computer.

It was after four by that time so I left Laura to deal with whoever Sam sent to pick up the mirror, took my film to a friend who does his own developing, and then headed on out to the Blue Owl again. Leaving that film reminded me

I hadn't brought in the two rolls I'd taken on the weekend. I made myself a mental note to put them in my purse when I got home. I was anxious to see how they turned out. Some of the scenery I'd shot had been gorgeous.

The same crowd was at the Owl. Allen dragged a chair around and made room for me beside his. They all greeted me as one of the regulars.

I ordered a diet cola, which Allen insisted on paying for, and listened to the numerous conversations going on around the table. They all knew about Sara but, surprisingly, no one seemed to think the two deaths were connected. After listening for a bit longer, however, I realized that wasn't strictly true. Allen was pushing the separatist theory, all right, and no one was arguing about it but I don't think they were all in agreement. They just didn't want to talk about the murders anymore. I couldn't say I blamed them; it was getting pretty close to home, but it made my joining them a waste of time. I was about to give up and make leaving noises when a tall bottle-blond in her late thirties gave me a sudden look of recognition and said, "Say, Demary, aren't you a P.I.?"

I did a swift mental check of what she might

know about me. "Nope," I said, mouthing my standard disclaimer. "I do research and genealogy. Although I do think I checked your references. You're Darlene Andrews, aren't you? Didn't you come over with TforToys?"

"Yes, so what do you mean you aren't a P.I.? Isn't that what they do, check references and stuff?"

I shrugged. "I guess so. Some do, anyway. I don't. The only reason I did TforToys is because it was for Carl. I did all kinds of stuff for him that I don't usually do."

Somebody snickered.

I gave the snickerer a sour inspection. Some people have grubby minds.

Darlene laughed. "Hey, Allen, did you know your references were being checked out by a licensed private investigator?" she asked in a joking tone, but there was something in her manner that suggested a threat.

"I didn't submit any references," he said, looking up from his beer. "Carl knew what I could do."

That was a flat out-and-out lie. I'd checked everyone of his references myself. But on the other hand maybe he was just indulging in some macho bragging. His credentials were impressive and probably would have assured him a job regardless of his references.

Laughter erupted at the next table. It was quickly hushed when Allen turned, scowling, but before he had a chance to speak the door opened and a noisy group of five came in. They were not from ETC. I recognized one of the women as a waitress named Carolyn from the Salmon House, a trendy and very expensive seafood restaurant at the south end of Lake Union where I'd had dinner a couple of times.

Carolyn broke away from the rest of her group and came over to our table. She stopped beside Allen and took a hold of his shoulder.

"Allen, do you know where Jon is?" she asked, sounding much more belligerent than the question warranted.

She was an extremely good-looking woman without being actually beautiful, with a figure most women would kill for. At the moment she was so irate about something she looked almost drab.

Allen shook his head, brushing her hand away. "No, I haven't seen him for a couple of weeks. Why?"

"He didn't come to work last weekend and if he doesn't show by tomorrow he'll be out of a job. I covered for him Saturday but it's Sea-fair week and we've been swamped every night. The boss is furious," Carolyn said, snapping the words out.

"You know him, he only works when he wants to. They won't fire him. He's the best maître d' they've ever had in the place," Allen said in a bored, almost rude, voice. He didn't look at her.

"He's good but he's not that good," she said, her face tightening resentfully. "If you see him tell him to check in if he wants to keep his job. I'm not covering for him again." She strode off toward her friends who had taken over a table in the back of the room.

"Oh yes she will," the woman next to me, Rosie, murmured in my ear. Rosie was one of those people who make the most trivial comment sound as if it were highly confidential information. She too had come to ETC from TforToys.

"Why not?" I murmured back, keeping my voice on the same level. We sounded like a couple of arch conspirators.

"She and Jon were a steady pair for a while. Six months or so, long enough for her to start thinking about wedding bells anyway, but I think he dumped her. I haven't seen them together for ages. She called him her blond hunk of love and she'd cover for him for a month if she thought she'd get him back.''

Something clicked in my mind. A blond hunk? Named John? Sara's current date maybe?

"What's his name," I asked. "John what?"

"North. And he spells his name J-o-n, not J-o-h-n. Jon North. He's a good maître d' all right but I wouldn't have him in the place if it was mine. He's stupid for one thing, and I do mean stupid. He doesn't have good sense. You can't depend on him, either. I know. Allen got him a job in my department at TforToys a couple of years ago. He only works as much as he has to to maintain his California tan and that boat of his.''

Blond hunk with a California tan? I had all I could do to *maintain* an indifferent pose. "What kind of a boat does he have?" I asked, taking a swallow of cola.

"A sailboat. Real old one, called the *Pacific Dreamer*. He lives on it. Ties it up at a slip on the west side of the lake near the restaurant.''

The guy on the other side of her, Allen's pal Bert, said something and she turned to him before I could ask her anything else, which was

just as well. It was entirely possible that whoever murdered Carl and Sara was working for
ETC and that someone could just as easily as
not be sitting at this table. I didn't need to call
attention to myself by asking too many questions.

I had no desire to be victim number three.

FOURTEEN

I EXPECTED ALLEN to say something about dinner. In fact I was wondering if I dared suggest the Salmon House, but he not only didn't ask me to dinner, he hardly spoke to me again. Leaving me miffed, to say the least. It wasn't that I had suddenly developed a flaming passion for him or anything like that; he was just a good-looking guy who seemed to like me and I thought he might be fun to have dinner with.

It didn't work out that way. He finished his beer and motioned to Bert and the two of them left a few minutes after Carolyn and her bunch came in. I wasn't actually disappointed but I was sure surprised. He'd come on strong the other time and I wondered why he'd changed. Surely it couldn't be because of what Darlene had said about my being a P.I. I didn't see how he could help but remember me. I'd talked to him personally about one of his references where he'd misspelled a name. Of course that had been several months ago and if I remembered correctly I'd just been getting over a horrendous bout with the Asian flu and looked like the wrath, but still?

Maybe I wasn't as unforgettable as I thought I was.

I left not long after he did. Bert Elder, Allen's pal, was standing on the corner talking to someone in an old Bronco. He gave a wave to a guy in an electric-blue pickup truck that pulled up behind me as I left the lot. The truck stayed on my bumper the whole way across town, crowding me. He tried to pass several times but the traffic on Eightieth was too heavy. I peeled off on Aurora and went around the north end of Green Lake, turning on Fiftieth to reach Corliss, the street in front of Werner's house. A half block away from it I saw Joey standing on the corner. He saw me at the same time and waved frantically.

I pulled up at the curb and waited for him.

"Hey, great, we're riding the same waves," he said, jumping into the passenger seat. "I just sussed out the two kids for you. The ones that found the body."

"You what!" I gasped. Sam would have my hide if he found out Joey was snooping for me.

"Don't worry," he told me airily. "Nobody caught on. The kids and Deana were playing in the yard so I wandered in and joined them. One of the kids' mamas was looking out the window and saw me. Never paid the slightest. Must not have a lick of sense.''

This last was said in a highly disapproving voice and I couldn't help but agree. Joey is slight and doesn't look his age but he doesn't look six either and a parent should have checked him out.

"No cop around?" I asked.

"Nope. I suppose the law figures they've already told all they know, but they're wrong. The kids saw the car drive in on Saturday morning. That's why they went and looked. Not because the dogs were barking. The dogs didn't start barking till after they found the body."

"They saw the guy?" I asked, flabbergasted. "On Saturday? And they never told the detectives? Why not?"

"Cops never asked. They're little kids. One, Tommy, was only six last month. The only dead person either one of them has ever seen was on TV and by the time the cops showed they were already so mixed up from everybody fussing at them they didn't know what they saw."

"Are they still upset?"

"Naw. I don't think they ever were upset, not really. It was like she was part of a movie. But they did see the guy and they might be able to pigeonhole him if you get me pictures of all the players and bad guys. I'll put a photo lineup together."

"Bad guys? You mean suspects? I don't have any suspects to start with and second, you can't do that kind of thing, Joey. I don't have any idea who the killer is. He could live right here in the neighborhood and could catch you at it."

"How's he going to catch me?" Joey asked, giving me a scornful glance from the corner of his eye. "I'm not that dumb. Nobody will be able to finger me. I'll do a game of it that won't have anything to do with the car they saw Saturday morning."

I frowned at him. "Saturday morning? Are they sure about the time?" If Sara's killer had left her body in the garage Saturday *morning,* that meant she had been killed not long after calling me.

"They don't know what time—they didn't have a watch, and they probably can't tell time yet anyway—but they do know it was Saturday because their dads were home and they know it was before they got hollered home for lunch.''

I sat for a minute, staring out the window, trying to fit times together.

"I nearly forgot—one of them, Tommy, is the one Werner gave his latest toy to," Joey said suddenly. "It was some kind of a gimmick where they could listen to what people were saying in the next room. Werner said it was going to be part of a spy game."

"Werner knew them? Did he know the parents?"

"Might of. C'mon, I'll show you. Werner's house is only down the alley from them."

Following Joey's directions I circled the neighborhood. Because of the Meridian playground this part of the district was cut up into irregular blocks. Some had alleys, some not, and some blocks were shorter than others. In this case, although they weren't all on the same block, nor even the same street, Werner's house, the orthodontist's, the two boys' houses, and the vacant property where Sara's body had been left were all within a stone's throw of each other.

I was about to let Joey back out—he'd left his bicycle in his little admirer's yard—when I remembered the toy and asked if the boy still had it.

Joey shook his head. "His uncle took it away from him."

I grinned. "Didn't like the idea of him overhearing things he shouldn't?"

"Naw, that wasn't it. He works for an outfit called HearAid. He said it might make a good hearing thing. You know, old guys like Mr. Madison put 'em in their ears."

I laughed to myself. I'd gone to Harry Madison's fortieth birthday party in January. He thought he was such a "with-it" guy; he'd really hate hearing himself referred to as an "old guy."

It was nearly seven when I got home. There were two calls on my answering machine but I didn't listen to them. I was hungry. They could wait till I'd had something to eat.

The kitchen was spotlessly clean, which immediately put me on guard. I had forgotten it was Wednesday, Nora's day to clean. She comes every two weeks. Some Wednesdays I find a sharp communiqué on a countertop warning me not to leave something—whatever she is annoyed about—in that condition again. But there was none today.

Nora had been working for my great-aunt when she died and after some consideration had agreed to give me a try. We were still on that basis. She was giving me a try. If it wasn't for her sending me a formal statement every six weeks of what I owed her—usually accompanied by an itemized account of what supplies she'd purchased on my behalf—I'd swear I worked for her, not the other way around.

The fridge was pretty bare but I finally concocted a pasta primavera out of fresh linguine, sautéed onions, tomatoes, zucchini, three tired mushrooms, a lot of olive oil, and a lot of garlic. It wasn't bad at all. Pasta is my downfall.

My phone messages, when I finally got to them, were all from Sam. He didn't sound mad so I poured myself a glass of my favorite white wine and called him back.

Sam and I really do have the oddest relationship. Sometimes he treats me like a younger sister, sometimes like a suspect, sometimes like another guy, but very very seldom like the woman he once asked to marry him. Tonight he seemed to be in the younger-sister mode. He had apparently forgotten our earlier confrontation—or had decided to ignore it—and had called to see if I wanted to go out to dinner.

Unfortunately I had already eaten so we settled on Friday, providing, as usual, that he didn't have to work. He even agreed to give the Salmon House a try, which was good of him as he doesn't like seafood and can get seasick just standing on the dock watching a ferry come in.

I went off to bed feeling as content as possible under the circumstances but I didn't sleep well.

Sara haunted my dreams. Like Laura, I couldn't believe she was gone. Sara had been a special person.

FIFTEEN

WHEN I WALKED IN the office the next morning Martha, with a face like a thundercloud, was just hanging up the phone.

"The cheek of that twit," she said angrily, scowling at me.

"I didn't do a thing," I protested. "Why are you mad at me?"

"It's that Dudley. The silly sod had the nerve to tell me you *had* to go. He said he'd given you a retainer so you *had* to go."

"Go where? To England? I never told him I'd go to England or anywhere else. What in the world is the matter with him?"

"He sounds like he's losing his mind is what's the matter with him. The man's bonkers. He was practically screaming at me."

"Well, forget him. I want you to access the ETC computer system. From here. I called Jean this morning and told her you were going to try to get into their system. She said to call her if you wanted her to do anything on her end."

"What are you looking for? And why from here?"

I ran my fingers through my hair, ruining whatever style I'd achieved earlier. "I'm honestly not sure. I just have a feeling I don't want any of the other people at ETC to know I'm searching at all. Whoever is responsible for Carl and Sara's deaths is sick, and I do mean sick. They *beat* Carl. I only saw the one picture of the crime scene but that was enough. I don't want to take the chance of anyone knowing that I'm even interested in the case. So you work from here."

She nodded.

I went on to tell her what to look for and then booted up my own system to work on Dudley's problem for a few minutes. The man irritated me but his problem was interesting.

Edward I of England reigned from 1272 to 1307. According to some accounts he had nineteen children, seven of whom were male, and most of whom survived infancy. It was one of the youngest, Edmund, that Dudley believed had written the letter found on his property.

To start with, I found it inconceivable that a letter could survive in readable form buried in the ground for over seven hundred years. Yes, according to Dudley, it was protected by a lead-lined casket, but I was still skeptical. However, I was being paid to find out if Prince Edmund could write at all and if he could have met the lady in question, not whether the whole thing was a scam. So I worked on the problem until nearly eleven and then took off for the HearAid Company where I'd had Martha make an appointment for me with the CEO. Which, incidentally, surprised the heck out of me. I had not expected Martha to get anyone to even see me much before next week, and certainly not the chief executive officer.

HearAid's offices were on Marginal Way south of the old Boeing Airport. My appointment was for one o'clock but the plant was in a heavily congested area, and with the Seafair festivities clogging all the downtown streets I wanted to give myself plenty of time to get there. It took me a while to find the place but it was still only twelve-thirty when I did, so I parked across the street to eat the burrito I'd picked up at a fast-food emporium on the way.

I was still peacefully chomping away when I saw Allen Johnson pull up at the intersection in front of me. A beautiful little brunette with a class-A figure got out of the passenger seat, then leaned back inside the car to give him what looked like a fairly passionate kiss. They talked for a minute, kissed again, and then she slammed the door and he drove away.

With her on tap no wonder he wasn't all that interested in taking me to dinner. I was curious how he had time to be here at this end of town at this time of day. How long a lunch hour did he take? ETC's plant was at the far north end of Lake Washington, another good forty-five minutes north of my office, and it had taken me nearly an hour and a half to get here.

My curiosity got a real jolt when the little brunette trotted down the block and went into the HearAid building.

But that was nothing compared to the jolt I got when the receptionist directed me to the CEO's office and the little brunette greeted me as his personal secretary. I darn near forgot what I was there for.

Mr. Baker, the CEO, greeted me pleasantly, if a bit uncertainly and I wished I'd thought to ask Martha what she'd told him I wanted to see him about. However, his attitude and the fact that he had been willing to see me on such short notice gave me a strong impression that he had something to hide. And all of a sudden I guessed what it was.

Hoping I was right, I jumped right in. No sense wasting time pussyfooting around.

"With Carl Werner dead and his office manager in the hospital, the situation at Electric Toy is pretty chaotic and I've been hired to help straighten things out," I said briskly. "One of the things we need to know is exactly what your agreement with Carl entailed."

He bought it—didn't even ask for identification, let alone authorization.

"Nothing illegal, I assure you," he said quickly. "We simply preferred to keep our agreement under wraps until he had the design perfected. Industrial espionage is as common in our industry as in any other."

"Was that the reason for the cash payments? Secrecy?" I was guessing on that one but he nodded without any hesitation.

"Yes, and as a matter of fact we gave him a substantial amount of money the Friday before he was killed," he said, looking glum.

"Ten thousand dollars?"

"Yes."

"Do you have any of the design specs yet?" I asked. "Had he given you anything at all?"

He shook his head no.

"Hadn't you asked him about them?"

He shook his head again but there was something a bit furtive in his expression that made me wonder if he was telling the truth. Paying out substantial amounts of money without getting anything at all in return didn't strike me as a good idea, but what did I know? Maybe that was how big business worked. There was nothing I could do about getting him to talk, though, so I decided not to press him for the moment. We talked a few minutes longer but I didn't learn much I hadn't already guessed. The uncle of the little boy who'd had Werner's listening device had brought the toy to his supervisor, who in turn had taken it to someone higher up, who had contacted Werner. Werner had agreed to adapt the thing to a hearing aid and to keep his work secret. HearAid had given him two payments of ten thousand dollars each, in cash, and they had signed an agreement, which HearAid had on file. All fairly straightforward and completely legal.

I thanked him for his cooperation, shook hands, and left well pleased with myself. Maybe I hadn't learned a lot this time but I'd be back. One of the things I wanted to know was why he immediately denied doing anything illegal. I hadn't accused him. He had been so nervous his hand was wet with sweat and I don't think he took a deep breath the whole time I was there.

He was hiding something for sure. But what? Was he mixed up in Werner's murder? And if so, why? If he didn't have the plans for the device yet, killing Werner—the goose that was due to lay the golden egg—would be nonproductive to say the least. And was Allen Johnson any part of it?

I tore up the interstate getting back to the office. It was a good thing I didn't encounter the state patrol. I couldn't wait to check my files on the employees that had come to ETC from TforToys. I was beginning to have a strong hunch that Allen Johnson had something to do with Carl's murder and I wanted another look at his references and background.

The motive for murder, in my opinion, usually fell into one of three categories: fear, gain, or accident. At the moment I couldn't see where any of these fit Allen, but maybe a fresh look at his résumé would tell me something.

I also wanted Martha to see what she could find out about the little brunette. I'd taken note of her name: Shirley McAfee. It sounded familiar, but I couldn't place it. Whatever, there was something about her knowing Allen that smelled of week-old fish.

SIXTEEN

MARTHA WAS BEAVERING AWAY at her computer when I got back to the office.

"I just pulled up the right directory," she told me. "Some of Werner's access codes are tricky but once you get the feel of how his mind worked they aren't all that hard to figure."

"Did you have any trouble accessing the system as a whole?"

"Jean put me in," she said absently, fingers flying across her keyboard. "She told me to tell you Connie is much better. Hey, here we are, the accounting program. What do you want to know?"

"Can you bring up the Friday before Sara… uh…" It hit me again. Sara had been murdered. This wasn't a computer game we were playing. "Look for a ten-thousand-dollar entry of some sort."

"Right here." She pointed at the screen. "No bank deposit, but ten thou was credited under miscellaneous income on Friday. And look what else I found." She keyboarded in another screen. "Werner not only had every phone in the office, the plant, and his home tied into the system, he had caller ID plus date and time. Look at this." She pointed again.

The screen held a list of numbers dated and timed Saturday morning. All were incoming to Werner's house.

"I've already located several of them," she said, sounding pleased with herself. "This one here is from the phone on the mezzanine of Sara's apartment building; this one, forty-five minutes later, is from the ETC offices as is the next one twenty minutes after that. And this one, at twelve-thirty, is from a call box on Westlake." She looked up at me expectantly.

"Uh, what...?" And then I got it. "Near where Jon North ties up his boat. Right?"

"Right."

"So Jon North, whoever he is, may be mixed up in it somehow."

"That's my guess."

"Carolyn, the woman who has been dating him, called him her blond beachboy."

"Sara said the man in her room was blond, and called him a California beachboy."

"Which doesn't prove a darn thing," I said regretfully. "But it's sure suggestive." I thought a minute. "Does that friend of Charles still have his boat down there?" Charles is Martha's husband. He's a professor at the university. He is a nice man but he's so vague he drives me berserk. Martha on the other hand is crisp and decisive. How the two of them ever got together is a mystery. Four or five years ago Charles got interested in boating—everybody in Seattle seems to catch that bug sooner or later— and bought a tiny little fifteen-foot cruiser with an outboard motor. They gave it up after one summer. Boating is a time-consuming hobby, neither one of them liked the constant care a boat requires, and Martha most definitely does not like being cold, wet, or dirty—conditions that seem to be an integral part of owning any kind of craft from a canoe to a frigate.

While they had it, however, they did meet some interesting people. One, an older man named Captain Tyson, had his boat tied up on the same side of Lake Union that Jon docked the *Pacific Dreamer* on.

"Yes, as a matter of fact Charles was down there talking to him last week," Martha said, making a resigned face. "Charles wants to go boating again."

"On Tyson's boat? The *Shady Lady?* You

must be kidding. As I remember it, the thing was as old as the Ark. Probably the only thing keeping it afloat was it was tied up to the dock.''

Martha grinned. ''It's not that bad, but no, Charles doesn't have a death wish. No, he and three other professors have the loan of a twenty-five-foot tug for a week and as none of them has the slightest idea how to work a boat, he wants Tyson to captain. The thing belongs to the oceanographic school. One of the men is researching something to do with whales. Orcas, I think.''

''Are you going?''

''Not hardly. Spending a holiday on a tarted-up old coaster isn't my idea of a good time.''

''I think I'll go talk to Tyson,'' I said. ''He should remember me.''

''That he should,'' she said, her eyes sparkling with remembered laughter.

The last, and only, time I'd been aboard the *Shady Lady* I'd tripped over something and knocked Captain Tyson into the lake. He hadn't been too pleased with me, particularly not, because I'd still been on deck. Lying on my belly, true, and with my head over the side, but *he* was in the water.

I studied the computer screen. "This doesn't do much for Borda's credibility," I said thoughtfully, putting times together in my mind.

"How so?"

"Borda claims the phone never rang on Saturday morning. Not as long as she was there, anyway. The phone rings in her room as well as the main part of the house so she certainly should have heard it. She says she left at eight-thirty. Not only is Sara's call timed seven-twenty, this one is even earlier. Who is it from?"

"It's from a cellular phone and I haven't had a chance to trace it yet. It's not listed in the local calling area."

An out-of-town cell phone—now that was interesting.

"All together there were five calls on Saturday morning," Martha went on, staring at her screen. "If your caller ID and time on Sara's call to you matches this one we have that nailed at least. The rest of the calls are guesswork as to who made them because they are all from public phones."

I paced back and forth, thinking. "I guess the first thing is to call Sam and tell him about the money. It provides a motive, of sorts, for the break-in and proves Sara didn't take it."

"He'll say it could be a double bluff. She could have entered it and still…"

"Yes, I know, and if it was someone else I might agree, but not Sara. She didn't think like that. Anyway, I'll tell Sam about it and about the calls Saturday morning. I don't know if he has paid much attention to Borda, although he did tell me he'd checked out her story of being at the parade. She and Millard met a friend at the Monorail station at nine o'clock."

Martha frowned. "Who…? Oh, the house-keeper. What motive would she have for want-ing Werner dead? She doesn't benefit under his will. Anna said the three women were the only ones mentioned at all."

"Who knows? Maybe she didn't think she got paid enough."

"She didn't," Martha said tartly. "Look at this." She had pulled up another screen with the payroll files on it and scrolled down to Borda's name. "Look what he paid her."

"Are you sure that's right?" I gasped. Carl had paid her by the week, minimum wage for forty hours. I'd be willing to bet the farm she not only worked twice that many hours, but that her kind of job was worth three times that wage. Jean was right. Werner definitely wasn't the jolly old toy-maker type.

"Of course I'm sure. That's what all her checks read," Martha said, giving me an offended glance. "It may not be the strongest motive for murder I've ever heard of but it's a darn good one. Talk about taking advantage of someone."

"I wonder why she didn't quit?"

"Probably because of the brother."

"Well, see if you can find out who has that cell phone. It at least should be a private party. And then find out what you can on Shirley McAfee. Don't waste too much time on her, though; she may not mean anything."

"Who is she? And oh, before I forget, Jean said Connie had been moved to a private room. I put the telephone number on your desk."

"That is great. I'll try to get down to see her before I see Captain Tyson."

I filled her in on what I'd learned at the HearAid Company, left her to do her thing, and went to pull my file on Allen Johnson.

As sometimes happens, the minute I had his file in my hand I remembered who Shirley McAfee was. She was Allen Johnson's cousin and had supplied one of his personal references. I'd talked to her on the phone. She lived in San Francisco, or had lived there at the time, and, if I remembered correctly, she lived in the same district as Laura Hope. I wouldn't have known it but Sara had recognized the address.

I flipped through Allen's file until I found her letter. She stated she had known Allen all her life, that he was hardworking, honest, trustworthy, blah, blah, blah, and so on. She gave her occupation as dental assistant.

And now, barely six months later, she lived in Seattle and was executive secretary to the CEO of HearAid? Talk about a fast worker. Too fast to be credible, particularly so considering the kiss she and Allen had shared. It hadn't looked like a cousinly kind of kiss to me. But then I have a suspicious mind when it comes to anything surrounding a murder.

I definitely needed to find out more about this lady.

SEVENTEEN

CAPTAIN TYSON WAS SITTING dockside on a pile of planking, smoking a cigar, when I walked down to where the *Shady Lady* was tied up. He remembered me.

"Well, well, if it ain't the detective gal with the two left feet," he said by way of greeting.

I made conciliatory noises and said I hoped he'd forgiven me.

He laughed, a huge booming laugh that startled a dozing seagull into taking flight. "Not the first time I got wet," he said. "Little water never hurt nobody, long as you don't take to drinking it."

I held up a six-pack of Oly I'd had the foresight to bring along and handed it over. He didn't waste anytime popping the tab on one and taking a long swallow.

Tyson was a big man and when young must have been well over six feet. His denim pants and shirt were clean but old and faded. As was the *Shady Lady*. Old and faded. The *Lady* had been seized in a drug raid ten years before and sold at auction. Tyson had bought her for the proverbial song and had lived aboard ever since.

"What brings you down here, gal?" he asked, wiping foam off his mustache. His pale blue eyes sparkled with humor.

"I'm hoping you can give me some information about another boat. I think the owner might…" I hesitated, changing my mind in midsentence. For all I knew Tyson and Jon North were bosom buddies.

"Might what?"

"Might be able to…uh…"

Tyson squinted at me. "Well, spit it out, gal."

Tap-dancing around wasn't going to get me anywhere; I might as well *"spit it out."* He couldn't do more than tell me to push off. "I'm looking for the *Pacific Dreamer* and Jon North. I think North may know something about a murder," I said bluntly.

"Wouldn't surprise me none. He's worthless—dumb, too," the captain said. "Who got murdered?"

I sat down on the dock and popped an Oly for myself. "One of my very good friends, and her employer, although not at the same time or in the same place.''

''What makes you think North had anything to do with it?''

''I don't know that he did but I'd like to talk to him,'' I said, squirming around until I could lean against a nearby bollard. There didn't seem to be any reason not to so I proceeded to tell him what, why, and all the rest of the story. He listened without interrupting.

''You ever seen North?'' he asked.

''No, never heard of him before this week.''

He stood up and held out his hand to give me a lift. ''Let's go aboard and I'll give you a picture of him. Took it a month or so ago when he was tied up on down a ways.''

''Here? He's been tied up on this slip?''

''Yep. Just three closer on shore. Been here for six months or so.''

Motor homes and boats never cease to amaze me. How the builders can cram so much into so little space is a wonder. Everything aboard the *Lady* was old and worn, but well cared for, and marvelously efficient. Tyson pulled out a shallow drawer under the table and removed a snapshot.

''I don't know the feller with him,'' he said,

handing me the picture. "He's down here with North every now and then. Not a sociable type, but then North ain't either. North is the one in the cutoffs."

The two men were standing on the dock with the *Pacific Dreamer* behind them. They were turned slightly away from the camera and seemed to be discussing something on the boat. North, dressed in nothing but cutoff jeans and a deep tan, looked like he should be riding a surfboard at Molokai. I didn't think I'd ever seen either of them before but there was something familiar about them.

"Can I borrow the negative of this?" I asked. "I'd like to get it blown up."

He shook his head. "Sorry. I never keep the negatives. Only have so much space aboard a boat. You can have that, though; I don't want it."

"Great. I have a photographer friend who can make a negative from this. You said North is usually tied up here. Do you know when he left?"

"Saturday sometime. He was gone when I got up."

"What time was that?"

"Well, to tell the truth, I didn't roll out till

after noon,'' Tyson said sheepishly, sounding remarkably like a ten-year-old. ''I had a couple beers too many the night before and it was close to one o'clock before I went on deck.''

''Out partying, huh? Wine, women, and song will get you every time.''

He laughed his huge laugh. ''Not quite— more like four beers, two old navy buddies, and listening to one another tell lies all night.''

''Does North usually stay out this long?''

''No. Fact is, I didn't think he was going out at all this week. Seafair is a big tip week and he's been talking about wanting to buy a blue-water sail. A boat big enough to make Australia. One he'll need a couple of hands to crew. That takes a bundle. He talked to me about going but like I told him, I never done any deepwater sailing and I already saw Australia.''

Bundle. The word triggered the memory of Sara using the same word when she told Laura about the money in the safe. What had happened to that money? Looking at the picture again reminded me of the mirror fingerprints. I still hadn't taken my other film in to be developed, either.

''Do you by any long chance have anything

of North's here?'' I asked. ''Anything that might have his fingerprints on it?''

''Fingerprints? Now how would I...'' He stopped, looking thoughtful. ''You wait.'' He disappeared up the little ladder to the cockpit deck. The boat rocked as he jumped ashore. A few minutes later he called to me from the dock.

''Get one of those plastic sacks under the sink and bring it up here.''

I dug out a sack and climbed up. Tyson held out two six-pack cartons full of empty beer cans and dropped them in the sack. He grinned impishly. ''I remembered North tossing these into that crate over there Friday afternoon. His prints are bound to be on them. Don't know who else's might be on 'em too, but that's your problem. You know you can't use 'em in court or anything, though. Obtained without his consent.''

''I'll worry about that when I know what I've got.''

I was more than pleased. I thanked him for all his help, promised to come back again when I had more time, and took off for home where I could dust the cans for prints, photograph them, and, hopefully, get them to my photographer friend before he closed for the day.

EIGHTEEN

WHEN I LEFT the marina I turned right on West-lake, went up the hill, and took the Aurora bridge across to Stoneway. By going home that way instead of going back to I-5 I thought I might miss some of the homebound traffic. I was wrong. It was bumper to bumper until I got to Wallingford and Forty-fourth, where I hung a left to go back to the office.

I had to use my key to get in. Martha locked up when she went home and the hall was dark. I should have left it that way because the minute I turned on the lights Harry Madison popped out of his office and I was trapped again. He had apparently been doing some kind of repair job around the place. He had a pair of pliers in his hand and a smear of dirt on his chin, but even in jeans and a grimy T-shirt he was his usual uptight self. He was determined I do something about our landlord, Ira Sharin, and no matter how many times I told him I either couldn't or wouldn't do what he wanted, he kept at me.

"Darn it, Harry, I've told you before, that's illegal," I said now in response to his demand that I put a tap on Sharin's office phone. Sharin had cleared out one of the small storerooms in the building and used it for an office whenever he was around. "And besides that, I don't know how to do a tap."

"Well, you could learn," he muttered. He started back into his office, then stuck his head around the door. "I heard about Sara. I'm sorry. She was a friend of yours, wasn't she?"

I stomped into my office and slammed the door. Sara had worked for him for ages. How could he be so casual? So uncaring?

Mentally consigning Harry to a hot place, I fired up my computer and started entering what I'd learned from Captain Tyson and then sat staring at the screen trying to sort out what I knew that might actually have some bearing on Sara and Carl's deaths. Taking them as one, because I was certain they were tied together in some way, there were only three people who benefited, or possibly only two. None of them could have committed the murders themselves and I couldn't imagine any of them even knowing how to go about hiring a hit man, let alone actually doing so. *I* didn't, and surely I'd know more about it than any of them.

So where did that leave me? Nowhere that I could see. The number-one motive in most murders was who benefited and in what way, but as far as I could see money wasn't a factor here. In Werner's case the three prime beneficiaries were Sara, Jean, and Connie. Or, if Sara died before Carl, Jean and Connie. Jean seemed to be out of the running as she was not at all pleased to be inheriting part of ETC. In fact, when I'd talked to her earlier she had said she would prefer not to accept her share at all but if she had to for some legal reason she would turn around and either give it to Connie or donate it to the Children's Hospital. I didn't know how Connie felt, but as she had been in the hospital the whole time she was out of it anyway.

With all three of them, of course, there was the possibility of their heirs, whoever they were, counting on getting the money. Unfortunately for that hypothesis I happened to know Jean had made out a will leaving everything she had to the Children's Hospital and although I didn't know how Connie had left her affairs I did know her only living relative was an elderly aunt who lived in North Dakota. I couldn't see either one of those recipients conniving at murder.

Laura benefited from Sara's death, providing that Sara did inherit. And Laura could be involved but it was pretty unlikely. They didn't need the money. According to Sara she and David paid more in income taxes than most people made to start with, and Laura was simply too devastated to be faking it.

I could not see any motive for Sara's death. It did not make any sense. She posed no threat to anyone and certainly had no enemies.

For Carl there were two possible motives. If, as Jean said, he fancied himself as a ladies' man, the killer could be an infuriated spouse, rejected ex of some kind, or even a current girlfriend. Unfortunately, however, the police hadn't found a trace of any such persons with any kind of a grudge against him. Another possible motive was Carl's latest toy. The listening device. Anyone of his toy patents represented money, a lot of money, and the so-far unpatented listening device could be worth millions.

As far as being physically involved, whatever the motive, in Werner's case the most likely

people were his housekeeper, Borda, plus anyone from ETC and/or TforToys, or a total unknown for that matter. In Sara's case there was
the man in her bedroom who might possibly be
Jon North, or again, a total unknown.

An interesting idea suddenly popped into my
head. Laura's husband, David, stood to gain,
too, if Laura inherited.

I wondered if he could be here now. Laura
had said he did the publicity for some of the
Seafair events.

The phone interrupted my thinking, which
wasn't going much of anywhere anyway. Not
surprisingly, it was Laura. That happens so often—a call from someone you are thinking
about—that it almost makes you believe in
mental telepathy.

She didn't give me time to say more than
hello and from her tone she was furious about
something again. She certainly had an unstable
temperament.

"Demary, do you know when the police are
going to release Sara's body? I'd like to make
some funeral arrangements. Anna says she
doesn't know and to ask you."

I thought some unkind thoughts about Anna Carmine.

"I have no idea, Laura. It depends on the medical examiner's findings and what bearing they might have on the prosecution's case," I said. I hesitated and then went on in as matter-of-fact a tone as possible. "You know she was strangled, manually, and they may still be trying to lift prints."

There was a long silence. "Yes, I knew. But I hadn't thought... All right, thanks."

"Wait, don't hang up. I've got a couple of questions."

"What questions?"

"I wanted to ask you if your husband, David, is in Seattle and if he by any chance had talked to Sara lately."

"No, he left yesterday. He's never around when I need him," she added in a sharp voice. "What makes you think he might have talked to Sara? He didn't say anything about seeing her recently."

"Nothing special," I said neutrally. Her tone bothered me. She sounded defensive, making me wonder. Several things she'd said left me with the feeling her marriage wasn't in the best of shape.

Her next remark didn't leave me in any doubt.

"I'm going to file for a divorce when I get back," she said abruptly, and burst into tears.

"Uh, Laura, would you like me to come over?" I asked, mentally kicking myself as I did so. I didn't want to hear about her problems. I had enough of my own.

"Yes, please," she sobbed.

"All right, I'll be there in about fifteen minutes."

WHEN LAURA ANSWERED the door to my knock a half hour later she was sober-faced but at least seemed to have recovered her poise.

I said, "Hi, Laura. Are you feeling better now?"

She said, "No, I hate him," and burst into tears again.

It took me a good five minutes to get her seated and calmed down enough to even understand what she was saying, let alone figure out what she was so upset about. As far as I could make out, during an early dinner that she had fixed for them here in the apartment, David had told her he would start going over ETC's financial records as soon as he got back from

New York, where he had a week of appointments scheduled that he couldn't get out of. I couldn't see anything wrong with that. A little premature maybe. He'd need to talk to Anna Carmine about it first, but on the other hand someone was going to have to do an audit, so it might as well be him.

She did not agree. "He doesn't care about Sara at all," she said, gulping back more tears. "He always resented my having her check our returns, so now he thinks he'll get even by going over all Sara's work and finding all kinds of fault with everything she did and criticizing her work and saying she should have done things different and saying she had cost ETC money and that she didn't know half of what she thought she did and finding—"

I stemmed the torrent with a glass of cold water. She took a gulp, looked at my undoubtedly anxious face—I didn't want to deal with another bout of hysterics like she'd had in the office—and broke into a series of chuckles interspersed with hiccups and little gasps of misery.

"I'm sorry, Demary. You must think I'm a total dimwit. You're certainly seeing me at my worst, actually a side of me I didn't know I had, but I just couldn't believe David could be so callous and then I got mad.''

''Mmm, yes. I can see that. But really, Laura, he may not have chosen the best time to bring up the subject but the probate court will require an audit and he is a CPA so I can't see—''

''I know. You're right,'' she interrupted. ''It was just the way he sounded, as if he couldn't wait to…'' She stopped, started again. ''He sounded greedy, like he couldn't wait to see what I was going to get out of it. Out of Sara's death.'' Her voice rose to a wail again.

Nine o'clock came and went before I finally got home. I never did get any dinner and as sorry as I felt for Laura I was beginning to think some of her marbles were chipped.

NINETEEN

I WALKED TO WORK in the morning, which wasn't as virtuous as it might sound. The office is only three blocks from my house. It was a beautiful day and I had a newish pair of knee-high walking shorts in a creamy apricot shade that went perfectly with a yellow plaid blouse I'd found in a thrift store a week ago. I love thrift shops. The big Goodwill store down on Dearborn is an absolute treasure trove of things people have discarded. It isn't that I'm cheap, or at least not very, but how could anyone resist a forty-dollar designer blouse for two dollars? I certainly couldn't.

Joey joined me at the corner. His outfit was exceptional, too. He was sporting a pair of cut-off jeans that were long past the ragged stage and well on the road to complete disintegration. Overall he wore a spanking new T-shirt two sizes too small for him in a gruesome shade of green with a printed saying that I wouldn't want to repeat. Someday I was going to have to ask him who purchased his clothes. And where.

"Talked to ol' Millard last night," he said, elaborately nonchalant. "He was out in the alley emptying trash when I went by. You ever seen the guy? He is one big dude, let me tell you."

"He didn't hurt you?" I asked anxiously.

"What would he want to do that for?" Joey asked, scratching a bony knee. "He ain't into that scene. And he's scared of his own shadow anyway. I never seen such a spineless custard." He shook his head somberly. "He shoulda clobbered that Carl."

"What? Why?"

"The toy guy was nasty. Millard hated him. Once he told Millard he had a surprise for him in the storeroom and when the poor guy went looking, Werner slammed the door on him and locked him in. No windows, and he knew Millard was afraid of the dark. Other stuff, too, with things that scared Millard. He told Millard they was just 'having fun.'"

I stared at him openmouthed. Lately, thinking back, I had realized I never really liked Carl very well but I had never suspected him of being sadistic. That kind of behavior put a different spin on things.

Joey nodded. "Not a nice guy. Still, killing

him wasn't a nice thing neither. Anyhow, did you get me the pictures?''

"No, no pictures. Not yet.''

"Well, get with it," Joey said severely. "I can't get much further without.''

"Joey, I don't want—''

"Catch you later," he interrupted, and tore off down the street yelling "Wait up" at another youngster.

I proceeded at a more sedate pace to the office where Martha greeted me with the news that she had uncovered some interesting information about friend Dudley.

"He's a sodding telly actor, and a third-rate one at that," she said, making a sour face. "And according to one of his mates, he's 'resting.' In other words, he doesn't even have a job.''

"That isn't exactly a crime," I said, puzzled. She made it sound as if he pulled the wings off baby butterflies.

"Where does an out-of-work actor get twenty-five-hundred dollars for a retainer? He can't pay his phone bill. Now I ask you, does that make sense? He's up to something and it's not likely to be an invite to the ball.''

"Hmm, you could be right, but until we

know what he is up to we'll just have to wait. In the meantime what, if anything, have you found out about Shirley McAfee?''

Martha scowled, irritated that I wasn't more concerned with Dudley, I suppose. At the moment his scheme, whatever it was, was low on my list of priorities. She pulled up a screen on her computer and doled out the pertinent facts.

''Shirley has worked for HearAid for eleven years, the last three in her present position. She is not Allen Johnson's cousin, nor any other relation. The one who lives at the address on the reference letter is her sister.''

Somehow I wasn't surprised.

Later I took the beer cans, dusted for prints, the picture of Jon North, and the film from my sailing trip over to my photographer friend. For once he wasn't swamped with work and said he'd try to get the cans done by the next afternoon. The rest when he could. I agreed, blew him a kiss, and headed back to my own neighborhood to have lunch at Julia's on Forty-fourth and Wallingford. I was hoping to get there before the noon crowd. Julia's is small and not fancy but they have wonderful food and they are always busy. I didn't manage to beat the crowd but I was in luck. Anna Carmine was already seated at a table for two. I joined her.

She looked spectacular in a cherry-red linen dress with a black bolero-type jacket. She gave me a brief welcoming nod.

I ordered pasta Marisole, a fabulous fettucine dish with artichoke hearts, sun-dried tomatoes, mushrooms, and pine nuts. I was tempted by the chicken in Dijon cream sauce but, as usual, pasta won. We chatted about nothing much until after it had been delivered, then, without telling her where I got the information, I told her what Joey had said and asked if she'd ever suspected Carl of being so nasty.

"No," she said, her face creased in a thoughtful frown. "No, I never did, but I never really cared much for him either. He was always perfectly okay with me but that business of insisting I come to the house rather than him coming to the office always struck me as a power play. I had the feeling it pleased him to inconvenience me. Did he ever do anything like that with you?"

I shook my head. "He did ask me to come over to the house a lot but I didn't mind. His place is only a few blocks from me. A couple of times he did ask me to do stuff I didn't like, things like checking out a competitor, but I just told him no.''

She gave me an amused look. ''Yes, I imagine you did. Why the interest in Carl's undoubtedly peculiar personality?''

''Have you ever met Millard?''

''Not met him, no. But I've seen him a number of times. Why?''

''I understand he's a big guy, very big, and it occurred to me that he had a very good motive for offing Carl.''

She didn't answer for a minute, her expression blank, then shook her head. ''He'd have the strength all right but he's too much of a child. I very much doubt he'd do anything like that.''

Joey did, too, but it was possible.

We finished our lunch in companionable silence. The dining room had cleared out some by that time. The tables around us were empty, so I asked her if she had time to answer a few questions about Carl's will.

''Sure. In fact, I don't have a single appointment this afternoon, so ask away.''

''If I have it right, the three beneficiaries had to be working for ETC at the time of his death. Yes?''

She nodded.

"But other than that, what?"

"Nothing. It's a ridiculously simple will considering the size of the estate, but he knew exactly what he wanted done and didn't want any advice from me. He leaves everything to the three of them providing they are still working for ETC, or the remaining two, or one. When I drew it up I protested that he was making no provisions for the possibility of all three of them being gone at the time of his death. He said he'd worry about that when there was only one left. There are no other beneficiaries."

"How does it stand now? Who inherits?"

"The three."

"But Sara's dead."

"We're talking about Carl's will. According to the medical examiner Sara was still very much alive at the time of Carl's death and she was still an employee of ETC, so unless she had something to do with his murder she inherited one third of the company."

"What will happen to her share now?"

"If her sister is correct about Sara's will her share will go to her, Laura. Nothing complicated about it. Of course Sara may have made

out a later will. I wasn't her lawyer so I have
no idea. That will be up to Laura to sort out.''

I told her about David saying he would go
over ETC's financial records.

"How ridiculous. In the first place, regardless of what we think, we still don't have any
assurance Sara wasn't involved in Carl's death,
but even if that was a positive, I haven't even
offered his will for probate yet. And when it
comes to an audit I'll hire one of the big na-
tional firms, not an independent.'' She snorted
with annoyance. "And certainly not one who
makes his living organizing foot races!''

TWENTY

I DECIDED I NEEDED to see Millard for myself so when I parted from Anna I headed for Carl's house.

Borda answered the door looking tired and depressed. Her gray-streaked blond hair was dull and scraggly, as if she hadn't bothered to brush it for days. She would have liked to refuse to talk to me, I could see it in her eyes, but when I told her I represented Carl's lawyer and handed her the note I'd had the foresight to get from Anna she finally let me in and led the way down the hall to the kitchen. The house was spotless, almost sterile feeling, and with all the curtains closed, most unwelcoming. I had an idea this was what Borda intended. The kitchen, however, was bright and sunny. A big man, I guessed to be Millard, was going out the back door as we came in. He was out of sight so fast I couldn't get a look at him.

"Was that your brother?" I asked quickly, turning to Borda. "I'd like to talk to him. Call him back, please."

"No." She stepped in front of the door, preventing me from following him. I thought for a moment she might actually shove me away. "No," she repeated in a fierce voice. Her pale blue eyes filled with tears. "You aren't the police; he doesn't have to talk to you. I don't want him anymore upset than he already is. You don't understand…"

For a second I thought of telling her he could either talk to me or he could talk to the police, but I changed my mind. As she said, I had no right to insist on talking to him and talking to her might be more profitable anyway.

"I'm sorry," I said smoothly. "I certainly understand, and I don't want to upset him, or you. I'll see him some other time. In the meantime I do have some questions for you."

Giving me a watery smile, she said, "Carl was so good to him. He thought the world of Millard. And Millard loved him, too. He misses him so. He just can't bear to talk about Carl."

A mistake on her part. Up till then I had considerable sympathy for her. Everything I'd learned about her denoted a decent, hardworking woman, grossly underpaid, who had spent her entire adult life caring for and protecting her brother. She didn't need to tell such a whopper. So why was she doing it?

I trusted Joey's judgment that Millard was too timid to have been involved in Carl's death, but that didn't mean Borda wasn't. And, in fact, from the available facts, it seemed very likely that she was involved in some way, or at least that she knew more than she had told.

"It must be awful for both of you," I said, putting on a sympathetic face. "Not only have you lost a good friend and employer, now you'll have to find another job." Crude, but she swallowed it whole.

"I'll never find a place as wonderful as this has been," she said piously.

We kept this kind of thing up for another minute or so and then I said, "I was wondering about Saturday when you came back from the parade. Didn't you try to check with Carl when you came in?"

"There were no lights on. I thought he was out. Millard and I watched a little television and went to bed."

That would have sounded reasonable except that Sam had told me she claimed she came back at around seven o'clock. It was still sunny and bright at seven; no lights would have been on anyway.

"So you were never here, in the main part of the house, from Friday evening until Sunday morning. Right?"

"Yes."

"And you stayed here in the kitchen until nearly nine o'clock?"

"Yes. I've already told the police all this. Why do you want to know what I did?"

I shrugged. "I don't, not particularly anyway. Like I said, I'm working for Anna Carmine on this. She wants to know what everyone did that morning and at what time they did it."

"I still can't see..." She turned and stared out the window.

"She says the timing is important. It has something to do with his will."

"I'm not in his will," she said with a sudden flare of anger. "He said he—" She stopped, almost in mid-word, and got up to walk across the kitchen. In a moment she started fiddling with some vegetables in the sink. "He said he'd leave me something," she said in an even voice. "But Miss Carmine says he didn't. Just as well he didn't, or people might think I killed him to get it."

I blinked my eyes, trying not to look surprised. The woman was either stupid or incredibly naive. She had just admitted to having a gold-plated motive if I'd ever heard one. She hadn't known until *after* Carl's death that he hadn't left her anything.

"What did he say he'd leave you?" I asked neutrally.

For a minute I didn't think she'd answer but she did, finally. "He said he'd leave me this house. So I'd always have somewhere to live and keep Millard with me," she said, her voice raw with pain.

What a total louse Carl had been. It certainly didn't say much for my powers of observation that I'd never even caught a hint of what he was really like. I found myself feeling very sorry for Borda. If she was telling the truth, and this did sound like the truth, she was getting a rotten deal. I decided it was time I changed the subject.

"Do you mind if I look around? I'd like to have an idea of the rest of the house. I've never seen anything but the front room and Carl's study."

She shrugged. "Go ahead. Doesn't matter to

me anymore.'' She gave a short burst of laughter. ''Doesn't matter to Carl either.''

There didn't seem to be any answer to that.

''Is that the door to the basement?'' I asked, pointing to a door on the far side of the kitchen near the outside entrance.

''I think it used to be. It's a small cupboard now.'' She twisted her mouth into the semblance of a smile. ''Carl had it boarded up and made the new stairs off the front hall.'' She got up and led the way. ''Come, I'll show you. Did you want to go down there?''

The ''new'' door to the basement was in the entryway opposite the arch to the living room. Right where Carl could keep an eye on it. The man had been obsessed with security.

I already knew about the stairs but I didn't think she was aware of that and I wanted to see how she reacted to my snooping around his workroom. She had been off shopping when Carl showed it to me. But for all the good that idea did me I might as well have stayed in the kitchen. She opened the door, turned on the lights, and went off, saying she had something she had to attend to.

The basement was as spotlessly clean as the rest of the house. It was divided into three enclosed sections with doors to each section in the small hall-like area at the foot of the stairs. The section on the left was the largest, holding mostly shelving and a furnace. The one in the center had more shelving and the laundry equipment. I took a quick look in both and then went on into Carl's phony work area, a good-sized room with all kinds of metal- and wood-working equipment. I say phony because although Carl did do a lot of work there, his important work—the toy designing—was done in the room concealed behind the trompe l'oeil painting of shelving on the outside wall.

I made sure the hall door was closed and then went over to examine the painting. It was so well done it was hard to see where the real shelves ended and the painting began until you were within a few feet of it. It didn't look as if it had been disturbed and I wondered if Sam had ever found the electronic key to unlock it. I'd have to ask him.

With Borda apparently uninterested in what I was doing there was nothing to keep me in the basement so I retraced my steps. When I got back upstairs Borda met me in the hall.

"Oh, there you are," she said, simulating surprise. "I thought you had left."

She may have been a good housekeeper but Borda was a poor liar.

"No, not yet. I'm going upstairs now." Suiting action to words I went up and took a look around. Sam's team had already gone over the place so I knew I wasn't going to find anything, but I wandered around for a while opening and shutting drawers and cupboards. Everything was squeaky clean and in its place, including, in the drawer of Carl's bedside table, the door opener for the shop behind the trompe l'oeil painting in the basement.

I stood staring at it for several seconds, astounded, before I realized why it was still there. With his usual deviousness Carl had designed the thing to look like a small tube of antacid. It even had a screw-off lid and space for several tablets. Anyone searching his belongings would never see what it really was. The only reason I recognized it was because he had deliberately shown it to me.

But when he showed it to me it had been on his key chain. How had it ended up in the bedside drawer?

I left it there and went over to stare out the window at the backyard. Borda was standing beside the garage coiling up a hose. I watched her for a while trying to decide whether to leave the door opener where it was or to take it with me.

I ended up leaving it.

TWENTY-ONE

SAM PICKED ME UP at six-thirty that evening. He looked quite dishy in a pair of dark green pleated slacks, a tan shirt, and a brown, crushed-cotton jacket. It was a gorgeous evening, still sunny, but cool enough to make a light jacket or sweater feel comfortable. I'd chosen an unstructured three-piece silk outfit in shades of yellow. We looked great together and set out in high good humor with each other.

He had made reservations at the Salmon House but we still had to wait for nearly an hour before we were seated. We spent the time in the lounge drinking a glass of Rhine wine and gossiping about mutual friends or acquaintances. Sam has a wonderful sense of humor when he lets it show, and despite his job he has a lot of faith in the basic goodness of mankind. When we were finally seated I saw Jon North's friend, Carolyn, scurrying around the dining room but we weren't in her section. Our table had a panoramic view of Lake Union. Boats of every size and description, including moored houseboats, lined the edges of the big waterway.

I pointed Carolyn out to Sam. "She is, or was, Jon North's girlfriend," I told him. "Have you found out anything about him?"

"Hmm, not bad," he said, taking an appreciative look at her. "Not bad at all."

"Well, have you?" I demanded, irritated.

"Have I what?"

I opened my mouth, ready to blast him, and only at the last moment realized he was putting me on. He could get me going every time, darn him.

"We did contact him, or rather we had the sheriff in Friday Harbor contact him. That's where he tied up after leaving here and he claims to have left Seattle before dawn on Saturday," he said, with an amused smile. "His fingerprints aren't on file anywhere and as far as I can tell he doesn't have anything to do with any of this. What has your sidekick found out about him?"

Sam and Martha don't care much for each other, mainly because both of them think the other bosses me around. Which strikes me as hilarious, especially so as I don't pay any attention to either of them. Sam, however, does have considerable respect for Martha's computer expertise.

"Just what I told you on the phone. The boat, the *Pacific Dreamer,* is registered to Jon North, but no car and, in fact, no driver's license. He has no address so we think he must live on the boat. He works here as a maître d', has no police record anywhere that she can find, and no record of ever being married. A lot of nothing."

He nodded. "We didn't find anything either. And there isn't a single thing to tie him to either murder. If he shows back up we'll talk to him, but that's it, Demary."

I started to tell him about the beer cans Captain Tyson had found for me but changed my mind. Sam still wasn't convinced of Sara's innocence so until I had proof positive that North had been the one in her apartment there was no use bugging him about the man. Instead I told him about Allen Johnson, Shirley McAfee, and the HearAid connection, and about Allen's black eye.

"We know about the black eye," he said, leaning back to give our waitress room to put down his salad. "But, unfortunately, not only does his friend corroborate the story of the car door, one of the box boys saw the accident, too, so there's no doubt it did happen. The kid said he took a heck of a wallop. Said half his face was black.''

"Did you know about the hearing aid thing?"

"Knew about it, yes. But at the moment can't see what it has to do with the murder. However, I'm not ignoring anything, Demary," he said in an indulgent tone, smiling at me.

I didn't trust myself to answer.

While we were eating our salad a couple of seaplanes came in and landed at the far end of Lake Union where the lake merged into the canal. One of the reasons Seattle is the fantastic town it is is that nowhere in the city are you more than a few minutes away from a lake, bay, river, canal, or some other waterway. That is also, of course, one of the reasons the per capita ownership of some kind of boat is the highest in the U.S.

Sam made appreciative noises as our waitress deposited our entrées. He had ordered a filet mignon with a side order of stuffed mushrooms.

"So you have no motive and no suspects," I said, taking a bite of my crab.

"I wouldn't say that. Regardless of what happened to the ten thousand Sara entered into the accounting system, I'm sure money is the motive for Werner's death.''

I shook my head. ''How, Sam? And who? Connie was in ICU and Jean was with her every minute of the time. I talked to three nurses and all say Jean was never out of sight from Friday evening until Sunday afternoon, and there isn't anyone else.''

''Except Sara.''

''She's dead! Or haven't you heard?'' I snapped. ''Darn it, Sam, money isn't the only motive in the world. Carl was a real jerk; there could be any number of reasons why someone else wanted him dead.''

''Who, and why?''

I told him about Carl promising the house to Borda, and about his other little peculiarities.

''No doubt he was an unscrupulous louse but I doubt very much that Borda killed him. We checked her story. She left the house at around eight-thirty, met her friend at the Monorail station, took her brother to the parade, and then went to a family picnic at Alki Beach. The family belongs to the friend she went to the parade with. She has no relatives here in Seattle. They were at Alki until six o'clock when one of the other people there drove them back downtown to where they could get a bus home.''

"All that alibi is good for is if he was killed Saturday morning after she left. Do you know for sure when he died?''

"Between two and four in the morning. That's as close as the M.E. can get it. I told you Carl was at his lady friend's apartment until after one, and that they had shared a bowl of popcorn at about eleven, so the time is fairly close.''

"Okay then, Borda could be involved. Why didn't she hear the phone? It rings in her rooms and his caller ID shows seven calls between six-thirty and nine.''

"Because her phone was out of order.''

"What? I don't believe it!''

Sam laughed. "Demary, as a detective you are the limit. Would I say that if I wasn't sure it was true? You talked to her this afternoon; why didn't you ask her about the phone? Werner himself reported her extension out of order on Friday morning. The phone company has a record of his call. They were supposed to check it out Monday but we canceled that work order and had it checked for ourselves.''

"And what was wrong with it?''

"The little plastic gizmo that plugs into the wall had a hairline crack."

"She could have done that herself," I said stubbornly.

He shook his head. "Not according to the lab."

I jumped from Borda back to fingerprints. I wasn't going to waste Sam's communicative mood on dinner conversation.

"Have you checked out all the fingerprints in the house?" I asked.

He nodded. "To tell the truth, there weren't all that many. I think that woman must spend half her time polishing the furniture. The only one not identified is a child's print on the plate under the back doorbell. It's probably one of the neighborhood kids. I understand several of them come over to see the brother, Millard."

"Whose prints did you find? Other than mine and Sara's?"

"A lot of ETC employees, including your friend Jean and the guy with the black eye. Johnson."

"Have you made any progress finding the couple who were in the elevator with Sara and the man in her bedroom?"

"So far, no."

"Darn it, Sam. Are you even trying?"

Sam put down his fork and leaned across the table to take my hand. "Demary, I've been working homicide for a lot of years. I know my job and you're ruining my dinner. Can we drop the subject. Please?"

Somewhat belatedly I realized I was ruining both our dinners. I do come on too strong sometimes. I had hardly even tasted my food.

"I'm sorry," I said contritely. "It's just that—" He raised his eyebrows at me, stopping me in mid-sentence.

"All right," I said, laughing now. "I'll be good. But only for this evening."

"Thank heavens. This steak is too good to waste."

We ate for a while in easy silence, then went back to some good-natured gossip. I finished my crab cakes, which were wonderful, and contemplated what remained of the glazed new-potato wedges that had accompanied them. I had already eaten half of them and if I finished the lot I was going to have to do an extra hour workout or I wouldn't be able to zip my jeans. Sighing mentally, I pushed my plate away. Martha could eat a whole pile of potatoes and never gain an ounce. It wasn't fair.

We had an especially pleasant evening, making me realize, again, how much I actually liked Sam. Plus, we had gotten through the entire evening without once really snarling at each other. In fact, by the time we got to my door I was feeling so mellow I asked him if he'd like to come in for a cup of coffee or something.

He said he would, and did.

TWENTY-TWO

I WOKE AT 2:20 in the morning thinking about Allen Johnson. Which irritated me. If I was going to think about anyone in my sleep it ought to be Sam. He had only left a short time before. Why should I be thinking about Allen Johnson anyway? And then, like a comic-strip character with a light bulb going on over her head, I suddenly remembered Monday night at the Blue Owl and Allen saying he had never been inside Carl's house. So how come the crime-scene boys had found his prints in both the hall and the kitchen?

He hadn't been testifying under oath, maybe he'd just said what he had because he didn't want to to be bothered with explanations, but why not simply say he didn't know, hadn't paid any attention? I thought about that for a while, trying to sort out who was lying about what and why, before I finally went back to sleep.

At 3:30 I woke up again still thinking about Allen Johnson. How had the bag boy at the supermarket known *half his face* was black and blue? There was no way his face would show that kind of bruising so quickly. The door accident had to have been a setup, a charade designed to be seen.

Or a figure of speech on the boy's part.

I dozed off sometime after the sun had turned my curtains a pale pink.

THE PHONE JOLTED ME out of sleep five minutes later. Or at least it felt like it was only five minutes.

"I'm sorry to wake you up, Demary," Sam said, not sounding one bit sorry. "I want to know when you left Werner's house yesterday, and if you saw Millard when you were there."

"Huh? When I did what?" My eyelids seemed to be glued together and for a minute I couldn't think what he was talking about. I didn't know anyone named Millard.

"Wake up, Demary!" His voice boomed in my ear, clearing my head with a snap.

"What? Okay, I'm awake. What do you want?" I looked at my bedside clock and then took a second look. No wonder I felt dopey. It was only seven-fifteen. With one thing and another I hadn't had much sleep. "What's going on?"

"I want to know when you left Werner's house and if you saw Millard," he said, every inch the homicide detective.

"I told you last night about being over there and about the door opener."

"I'm not interested in the door opener at the moment, although I did tell one of the uniformed men to secure it. What I want to know is when you left."

"I don't know. About three-thirty, I think. What difference does it make?"

"She's gone. One of the neighbors called the local precinct. He works nights at the Northgate hospital. Ten at night to six in the morning. His garage is on the alley behind the houses and when he passed the back of Werner's he saw that the kitchen door was standing wide open. Said it bothered him because of the murder, so after he put his car away he went over to check. He knocked and rang the bell, and when no one answered, he decided to call in."

"What happened...I mean, she isn't dead, is she?"

"No. At least not as far as we know. Her car is gone and from the looks of things she packed up everything she owned, possibly even a few things she didn't own, and left sometime not long after you were there. In fact, now that I think about it, that's probably how the door opener got into Werner's bedside table. She very likely took a couple of the toy prototypes with her. So, when did you leave?''

I rubbed my eyes, trying to wake myself up a little more. I'd gone back to the office after I'd left Borda but I couldn't remember looking at my watch until sometime later. "I don't know, Sam," I said eventually. "I just never paid any attention. Martha might know though. I went straight back to work and the house isn't five minutes from the office.''

"I'll talk to her.''

"But what about Millard? The boy, or really man, I guess.''

"Did you see him yesterday?''

"Yes, but just for a moment. He…'' I stopped, remembering. I had only had a glimpse of his back as he went out the door. I had never seen Millard so I had no way of knowing if the man I saw was him or not. I told Sam.

"His clothes are gone, too, so we're presuming she took him with her.''

"There isn't any reason why she couldn't go if she wanted to, is there?''

"She was told not to leave town without informing us."

I couldn't help giggling. "Do you mean everybody doesn't do exactly what you tell them to do?" I asked, teasing.

He sighed. "Demary, look alive, will you? You know better than that. She's a possible suspect in a murder case."

I did know that and the thinking I'd done in the small hours of the morning had convinced me she had to know more about Carl's murder than she'd told. A lot more. I'd walked around the yard after I left her yesterday and the way the house was built there was no way she wouldn't have heard what went on in the living room regardless of whether she was in her own part of the house or not. Werner wouldn't have taken that kind of a beating in silence. But whether she'd kept quiet and stayed away out of self-protection or malice was anybody's guess.

Millard had told the little girl, Deana, that Borda locked him in his bedroom sometimes. I wondered now if maybe Borda had a boyfriend, if after Millard was safe in bed she sometimes went out. If so, that might be where she had gone now, and might also be why she hadn't heard anything the night Carl was killed. Sam said he'd check it out.

After we hung up I dragged myself out of bed, put on a pot of coffee, and while it brewed took a steaming hot shower to wake myself up. I never could see the cold-shower bit. It might sound attractive if you were into masochism, but in practice it would very likely give you a coronary.

I had finished what few household chores I forced myself into doing and was getting ready to go grocery shopping when Mrs. Ireland called.

"Good morning, Demary," she said briskly when I answered. "I have some news for you. I've found the couple who were in the elevator with Sara. Mr. and Mrs. Peters."

"What? How in the world did you find them?"

"I went over to the senior center and asked," she said complacently.

"Oh, my goodness." I gasped, not sure whether to be delighted or horrified. "I hope you were careful who you talked to." The thought of Mrs. Ireland trotting around asking questions tied my stomach in a knot.

"Of course I was," she said in a dry, don't-try-to-teach-your-grandmother-how-to-suck-eggs tone. "The Peterses have been gone for a while, visiting relatives in Yakima, so of course they didn't know anything about Sara's death." She paused, then went on. "They are planning to leave again tomorrow morning so if you want to talk to them it might be a good idea to come over as soon as possible."

"Could you call them or something and ask if I could come right now?

"I'm in their apartment; it's number 3-C. We'll wait right here for you." She hung up without waiting for me to answer.

I couldn't help grinning. Nothing slow about Mrs. Ireland. As she said, she might be seventy but that didn't mean she was senile.

I was ready to go out anyway so it only took me a couple of minutes to find my purse and head out the door.

Joey was sitting on the porch steps. "'Morning," he said, standing. "Thought I'd help tote your groceries."

"How did you...Oh."

Joey nodded. "Saturday mornings."

"I'm going somewhere else first," I said, thinking it might not hurt to take Joey along. "But you can go with me if you want to. I'm going to see a lady named Mrs. Ireland. She lives in the Eastview apartment complex.''

''Where Ms. Garland lived.''

''Yes.''

''Let's get with it, then.'' He opened the car door for me before vaulting over the rear fender and getting in on the passenger side.

AS I THOUGHT MIGHT BE the case, both the Peterses and Mrs. Ireland took to Joey immediately. He has some kind of a built-in rapport with older people. His presence definitely eased the Peterses' initial nervousness at having to talk to a *private investigator*. Their italics, not mine. But even at that the conversation didn't go too well.

After some opening courtesies—the Peterses were the kind to expect them—my first question was, did they know the man? Had they ever seen him before?

''Oh no,'' Mrs. Peters said. ''He was rude.''

''Uh, oh, that wasn't exactly what I meant,'' I said, hoping I didn't sound impatient. ''But how do you mean, rude? Did he say something or was he forcing Sara to accompany him?''

She turned to her husband. ''I don't think so, do you, William?''

"Must have been," he said, smoothing his moustache. "Got away from him smartly enough."

"Well, yes, that's true," she said, thoughtfully. "But she could have asked for help, told us she didn't want to go with him."

Looking at the two people sitting on the couch in front of me I could see why Sara hadn't said anything to them. Both of them were well into their eighties. Sara wouldn't have wanted to involve them.

They tried, the two of them, to tell me exactly what they remembered about their encounter with Sara and the unknown man, but even with the side issues Mrs. Peters included, such as the man's too-tight trousers, "really quite offensive, dear," it wasn't too informative.

"Can you describe the man?" I asked finally.

That they could do. They couldn't, however, add much to what I already knew. He was tall, had blond hair, a dark tan, and bright green eyes.

"You need pictures," Joey muttered *sotto voce*.

"What's that, dear?" Mrs. Peters asked.

"Pictures? Yes, that would be helpful wouldn't it, dear?"

Joey smirked. He patted Mrs. Peters's hand. Mrs. Peters beamed.

I swore to myself. How in heck was I supposed to get a picture of someone I didn't know and couldn't find? On the other hand I did have a picture of Jon North and a strong suspicion he was involved. I needed to see my photographer friend before I did anything else.

TWENTY-THREE

MRS. IRELAND ACCOMPANIED Joey and me to the building entrance where we met Laura Hope on her way in.

Laura gave Joey's shirt an astonished look but managed not to say anything. Fortunately neither the Peterses nor Mrs. Ireland had seemed to understand the significance of the bizarre little drawing on the front and its accompanying text.

"I feel like I already know you," Laura said after being introduced to Mrs. Ireland. "Sara spoke of you so often."

Mrs. Ireland voiced appropriately sympathetic phrases and added that she had been very fond of Sara. "She was a really sweet person."

"Thank you, I loved her very much and I'm going to miss her terribly," Laura said, blinking back her ever-ready tears. She turned to me. "I'm glad I ran into you, Demary. I was going to ask if you would go with me out to Sara's house. I'd like to see it, and maybe you would like to go also, Mrs. Ireland? I've hired a car and can pick everybody up at whatever time is convenient.''

"How about sometime tomorrow?" I asked. "I can't make it today."

They both said that would be fine and we agreed to meet in front of the apartment at one o'clock the next day. We talked for a few minutes, then Joey and I took off for the U district where my photographer friend had his shop.

He wasn't there. "He went out of town on a, uh, family emergency, uh, kind of thing," the young high school student he'd left in charge said.

"I developed your two rolls of film," he added, holding out a fat envelope. "I know how to do that but Marty told me not to touch the other stuff. He said he'd do them the very minute he got back."

"Darn. How long is he going to be gone? Did he say, or does he know?" I asked.

Joey looked embarrassed. The boy stared at me as if I had two heads. "I think the emergency will be over by Monday morning," he said, with a knowing leer in Joey's direction.

I jerked the envelope out of his hand and

stomped out the door. Teenagers thought they were entirely too smart.

My pictures were even better than I'd expected. Some of my shots of other boats as we drifted along the coast of the Sound were really great. One of Carol Ann leaning against the rail was particularly nice with a passing sailboat in the background and the water sparkling like diamonds. Joey looked them over twice and pronounced them totally smooth. I assumed that meant they were good.

JOEY WAS SITTING on my front porch again when I went out to get in my car the next morning. Dressed in a very respectable pair of new jeans, a plain navy-blue golf shirt, and clean new Nikes, he looked a regular Norman Rockwell, Sunday school boy.

"Mrs. Ireland invited me," he said, sounding surprisingly unsure of himself. His change of apparel seemed to have dampened his personality some.

"Fine with me," I said, ignoring his wardrobe.

Beaming, Joey got in the car.

LAURA STARTED CRYING again the minute she pulled up in front of Sara's little house. This time, fortunately, it was only a gentle weeping, no hysterics. She sat for a while just looking, then after a bit got out and walked up the path. Mrs. Ireland walked alongside her murmuring words of sympathy and comfort.

Laura didn't have the keys; she had forgotten to get them from Anna who had collected them from the broker's office. The sale had been completed so I supposed the house belonged to Laura now.

"Maybe the back door is unlocked," Joey said cheerfully. "I'll go look." He raced around the side of the house and minutes later opened the front door to let us in.

I gave his dusty shirt a thoughtful inspection. The back door had been very securely locked on Tuesday. I'd tried it myself. He gazed back at me blandly and took Mrs. Ireland's arm to help her up the steps.

The inside was still empty and draped with cobwebs but it was easy to see why it had appealed to Sara. The floor plan was what I think is called English Cottage design, with a small central hall, two bedrooms and a bath on the left, a nice-sized living room, dining room, and small kitchen on the right. All the floors were hardwood.

"It's really nice, isn't it?" Laura said, wiping her eyes. "Sara was so happy with it."

Mrs. Ireland patted her hand. "You know, Laura, I don't think this is such a good idea after all," she said gently. "I know you had to see the house but I don't think we should linger. There's nothing you can do here and it's just making you feel worse."

Laura nodded. "Yes, you're right. I didn't realize...I'm sorry I'm being such a weepy thing. I just can't..." She squared her shoulders. "Yes. Let's leave. I'll tell you what." She gave us a damp smile. "Why don't we go somewhere nice and have an early dinner. My treat."

"That sounds lovely," Mrs. Ireland said. "Demary, do you have any suggestions? Joey, where would you like to go?"

"The Space Needle," Joey said promptly. "The food's good and the view is fan-tas-tic. Take your mind off things, Ms. Hope."

I blinked. Joey was a constant surprise. The Space Needle was pricey, sophisticated, and I would have thought well beyond Joey's experience. I was obviously wrong. It was a thoughtful choice. The view would definitely take Laura's mind off her loss, for a little while at least. The revolving restaurant atop the Needle let one view the entire panorama of not only Seattle itself, but also Puget Sound, the canal, several lakes, and both of our mountain ranges—the Cascades and the Olympics.

Mrs. Ireland had never eaten there so it was a doubly good idea and we got back into the car in a more cheerful mode.

Laura swung onto I-5 and we were just passing Boeing Field on our way back into town when Joey gave me a sharp poke in the ribs.

"Look," he hissed. "That psychedelic blue pickup in the next lane over. Look quick. I think that's the truck that creamed Mrs. Black."

"What?" I whipped around trying to see past Laura's shoulder. She and Mrs. Ireland were in front. I could just see the right side of the pickup but not the license plate. It was two cars ahead of us and going faster than we were. "Are you sure, Joey?"

"Not positive, but I think so."

"Laura. See if you can catch that blue truck ahead of us on your left," I said softly, not wanting to startle her.

Laura obediently made an effort to speed up but the traffic was so heavy it was impossible.

She switched lanes and gained a few yards, then lost it again as the truck wove in and out of the traffic ahead of us. "What is it?" she asked. "Why do you…"

"Joey says he thinks it's the pickup that hit Connie. Try to come up behind it so I can get a look at the plate."

"How can you know for sure?" Laura asked, glancing at Joey in the rearview mirror.

"It's got a heavy strap-iron grille, a custom-made job, and a cracked shield," Joey said sharply. "If we can see the front I'll know for sure whether it's the right truck."

Laura tried her best but the traffic was too heavy. We were still in the far left lane when the pickup signaled a right and disappeared down the Dearborn off-ramp. We were past the turn before she could change lanes.

Joey sat back with a sigh. "I never did get a good look," he complained. "But I did see the back of the guy's head. Big guy with curly blond hair."

"That's more than I saw," I said. "Did you see the driver, Mrs. Ireland?"

She shook her head. "No, but I do think I've seen the truck before. Parked on a side street near the apartment. Or one like it. That color. It practically hurts the eyes.''

"I think it may be a fairly common paint job. There was one the same color behind me the other night when I left the Blue Owl. You really think it's the right truck, Joey?''

He nodded judicially. "Yep.''

"Then we need to talk to Jake Allenby. He's handling Connie's case. I didn't see the grille myself but if you're right, Joey, the grille is why there were no paint residues from the truck on Connie's car. I wish we could have gotten the plate number but even that much description may help. But why in the world didn't anyone else see that grille?''

"Probably cause they was looking from in back. Mom and me was on the other side of the lot. I was looking more from the front. No one else was over where we were. Mom parks back there 'cause she ain't too good a driver. Lots of room on that side and she doesn't have to worry about backing into anyone.''

I called and got a hold of Jake while we were waiting for a table—which, incidentally, we got with record speed. Joey knew the maître d'. Jake placed the description within minutes. A

pickup answering that description had been stolen the same day Connie was hit in the supermarket parking lot.

TWENTY-FOUR

WHEN I GOT HOME that evening the first thing I did was call Joey's mom and apologize for keeping him away so long. She was very nice, assuring me it was perfectly all right as Joey had called her from the Space Needle and told her where he was. She didn't seem at all surprised that he should have been having dinner at one of Seattle's more renowned eateries.

It wasn't late, not yet dark, so I changed into an old pair of sweats and went out in the backyard to look at my little fish pond. I do not like yard work. I hate grubbing around in the dirt so most of the backyard is brick and tile with a few ornamental trees in big pottery tubs. The fish pond is different. It's about as big around as a dining-room table surrounded by a raised tile lip that invites sitting. I get a big kick out of the goldfish, or as the Asian gentleman who owned the aquarium shop called them, the golden carp. There are six of them and I swear they know me. The minute I show up with the container of fish food they come to the top and start blowing bubbles at me.

I sprinkled their dinner on the surface of the water and sat watching them dart around after the tiny nuggets as I thought about the people involved in the two murders, their connections to one another, and how they fit into the pattern I was struggling to put together in my head. None of the bits and pieces I felt sure of wanted to mesh with anything else. Too many pieces seemed slightly out of place, as if my premise was skewed, out of focus in some way.

Carl had to have admitted his killer into the house himself. The security hadn't been breached and after thinking over my meeting with her I couldn't see Borda as the instigator or even as a part of any kind of conspiracy. She didn't have the intelligence. I still thought she was hiding something but doubted now if it had anything to do with Carl's death. Which meant Carl must have known his murderer; he was too security conscious to have let a stranger in at one o'clock in the morning. In fact, I doubted if he would even have opened the door to a stranger. Both his front and back doors were equipped with closed-circuit cameras and he would have definitely taken a good look at anyone on his porch at that hour. So who would he have invited in at that time of night? A woman maybe?

It was highly doubtful that a woman could have done the deed herself but once inside the house she could have opened the door to someone else. Although more and more women were learning karate nowadays, and Sam said the M.E. was almost positive one blow to the side of Carl's neck had been a classic karate chop. That hadn't been what killed him, however, so theoretically, at least, a woman could have been responsible.

But what woman? Sara was, I had to admit, the most likely candidate for being allowed into the house, but I still didn't believe she had anything to do with his death. Connie and Jean were out of it, or at least Connie was. Jean could have left the hospital during the night and gone to Carl's but it was highly unlikely. So what woman was left? Laura? Farfetched to say the least. If she had any part in her sister's death, she was an Oscar-winning actress.

Not a woman then. What man would Carl have asked in? A friend? Yes, possibly, but Sam had had all his friends checked out and although none of them had absolutely airtight

alibis for that time of the morning it was extremely doubtful that any of them were guilty.
Someone from the plant? Yes, again, if he knew
the man well and he thought there was good
reason. And that was the stumbling block. I
could not think of a single male, employee or
otherwise, that he either knew well enough or
would have trusted enough to allow in at that
time of the morning. Carl was simply too paranoid.

My next problem was motive. Who benefited? His will certainly made that clear enough,
but there again my mental pattern hit a snag.
None of the three beneficiaries could have had
anything to do with his death. The missing ten
thousand dollars might be motive enough for
Carl's death if he had gone back to the office
and put in his wallet or taken it home. But in
that case where did Sara's death fit?

Which meant there had to be another motive.
Who either hated or feared Carl enough to kill
him? And why?

I went inside and went to bed. Maybe Sam
was right. I was a lousy detective.

I WAS LATE getting to work. I had constructed
an entirely new theory in the small hours of the

morning and I tested it out as soon as possible by calling Mr. Baker at HearAid. He confirmed one of my deductions but completely blew the accompanying surmise, leaving me back where I started.

I didn't even have to lean on him to get him to talk. In fact, he was so eager to get it off his conscience, he fell all over himself in his haste to get the words out.

Allen Johnson, probably through the auspices of his girlfriend, Shirley McAfee, had approached Baker not long after the boy's uncle had first taken the hearing device to his supervisor. He told Baker he could get the plans for him, for a price of course, and Baker had agreed. He hadn't produced them, however, and Baker had gone ahead with his deal with Carl. He claimed he'd had second thoughts, decided he didn't want to be involved in anything illegal, but I found that hard to believe.

Allen hadn't told him how he was going to get the plans and for a bit I wondered if he was responsible for Carl's murder in an attempt to beat the plans out of him. But there again I hit the same stumbling block. Carl would never have let him in the house at that time of night.

It looked as if Allen was no more than a cheap crook, and an unsuccessful one at that.

WHEN I GOT TO the office I found Martha sizzling with anger. Even her body language was hot.

"Do you know what that beastly Sharin did?" she demanded, stomping into my office behind me.

"Sharin? No. What has he done now?" I asked, confused. Martha had always been more amused than anything else by the Sharin controversy. I dumped my purse on a chair and went around my desk to sit down. The way she was jittering around I wanted something sturdy between us.

"He hired Dudley!" She paused, waiting for my reaction.

"He did? What for?" I stared at her doubtfully. What possible work could Sharin have for the man? And why should Martha care? Maybe whatever it was would get Dudley out of our hair. He had called again Friday afternoon.

"Not now, you idiot. He hired him two weeks ago. To get you out of town."

It took thirty seconds for all the aspects of that to sink in. "You mean…you mean Dudley doesn't have...you mean the whole story was a scam? Sharin simply wanted me out of the way so he could work on the other tenants?" I asked, beginning to simmer myself.

Martha nodded owlishly. "Yep."

"Harry's right. The man's crazy. I'm no threat to him. Unless he's planning something sneaky."

"Yep."

I swore. "I spent hours on that darn research," I said, furious.

"Yep."

"Well, he's going to pay for every minute of my time, blast him. Every single minute. Type up a statement and send... No. Hmm, let me think." I sat for a minute, gazing into space. "Okay, get the bill ready but don't send it out," I told her slowly, still mulling over the perfectly delicious idea I'd come up with.

"Are you going to let Sharin get away with this?" Martha demanded.

"Not if I can help it. But first, what about Dudley's check? You haven't deposited it yet, have you?"

Martha shook her head, not happy about that either.

"Well, do it right away—make sure the darn

thing is still good, then we'll see. How did you find out about Dudley anyway?''

''I saw them talking together Saturday morning. Sharin and Dudley. On the street over in the U district. Them knowing each other struck me as dodgy and got me to thinking. So I called a girl I know in one of Charles's classes. Helena Ames. She's a drama student. I asked her if she knew him or knew of him. She didn't, she goes around with a much younger group, but she said she'd talk to some of the others. No one knew him but one of the older girls in her drama class suggested she try a coffeehouse she knew of down on Second. It's apparently a kind of meeting place for wannabe actors. So Helena decided to give it a try.''

''Saturday? This was on Saturday?''

''I talked to her Saturday evening. She and a girlfriend went there yesterday afternoon, asked the waiter if Dudley had been in lately, and the next thing she knew everybody in the place was telling her all about it.'' Martha took an angry breath. ''The whole bunch not only knew about it they thought it was hilarious. One man actually said it was the best gig poor old Dudley had landed in ages. The only problem was that Dudley hadn't been able to get you out of town yet and his employer, Ira Sharin, was getting anxious.''

I scowled. ''They actually said it was a setup? To get me out of town?''

''They did, and they thought it was funny.''

Them thinking it was funny was apparently what was infuriating Martha more than anything else. Well, I'd need to talk to Anna first, but then we'd see how funny Sharin thought it was.

But first I had a murder to think about. This business with Sharin and Dudley had put a whole new notion in my head.

TWENTY-FIVE

I CALLED MY photographer friend to see if he was back and if he'd finished my pictures. He had, so I went over and got them right then.

He may have taken the weekend off but Marty had done a spectacular job of photography when he got to it. He had shot every can in three or four positions, then isolated each and every fingerprint on its own, labeling each individual picture with a number corresponding to one of the numbers he'd put on the can pictures. There were forty-two photographs in all.

I'm not particularly good at print comparison and with that many individual sets it took me three hours just to sort them out. The same fingerprints were on a lot of cans and when I laid out the set of pictures I'd shot of the mirror fingerprints I hit the jackpot almost immediately. I had a match on seven beer cans.

The next question was whose prints were they? There were four different sets of fingerprints on the cans and no way at the moment of telling which ones belonged to Jon North.

I had no choice. As much as I hated to do it I'd have to pass this on to Sam. I didn't have the resources to follow it up.

Predictably, he was not happy with me but he was too busy to do more than snarl as he said he'd send someone out to pick up the pictures and the cans and for me to have them ready. I could hear a voice yelling for him in the background.

Speaking in my meekest tone I said I'd have them all packaged up and waiting. For some reason he didn't seem to buy meek. He hung up without saying good-bye.

I put the whole lot, except for the blowups of Jon beside his boat, in a box and took it out to Martha. I told her not to let anyone bother me for a while and went back to my own desk to do some thinking.

After a while I got the snapshots I'd taken from Jake's boat out of my purse and sorted out the one I wanted and laid it beside the one of Jon North. I was looking at the same boat. And as much as I hated to admit it I was beginning to believe I'd been taken in by another performance, a charade of tears.

The phone rang but I didn't bother picking up. Martha would catch it in front.

A minute later Martha came in. Her beautiful chocolate-colored face was almost gray with shock.

"What is it? What's wrong?" I gasped, jumping to my feet.

She sagged against the door frame, her hands clutching at air. "The p-phone..."

The phone call had been from Sam. He had called to let us know that Laura Hope was in ICU and not expected to live. She had been attacked in the apartment parking lot, apparently by a mugger.

Another tenant, driving into the lot, had seen what was going on and had raced toward them, horn blaring. Laura's attacker had run, disappearing into the shrubbery before the man in the car could reach them. Williams, the man in the car, had stayed beside Laura, used his cell phone to call 911, and had undoubtedly saved her life. She had been hit at least three times with the sand-filled stocking the mugger dropped as he fled. The first reports from the emergency room indicated that her cheekbones and nose had been broken; her shoulder, the back of her neck, and her upper spine had sustained major damage; and her skull had probably been fractured.

"A m-m-mugger?" I stuttered, unable to take it in. This couldn't be right. Muggers were smash-and-grab experts; they didn't assault their victims that way.

"Sam said he took her purse." Gulping—the gray was beginning to take on a green tinge—she turned and ran down the hall toward the rest rooms.

I didn't feel too well myself.

"Sorry," she said when she returned. "My own fault. I should have put him through to you but I told him you weren't here so he gave me the details, and he described her condition pretty graphically. The sod."

"Did he say how..."

"He said for you to call him. Let him tell you," she said. "I don't want to think about it for a minute." She went out, still looking shaky.

My first question when Sam answered was, when did it happen?

"Last night. Seven-fifteen almost exactly," he said. "Williams's 911 call came in at seven-eighteen and he says he jumped out of his car and took a look at her before he punched in the number."

"But...but...I...we...How could it? I didn't

leave there until seven o'clock. I know. I looked
at my watch because of Joey. What happened
to Mrs. Ireland? She wasn't hurt, too, was
she?'' I could hear my voice rising to a regular
screech.

"Demary, calm down," Sam said sharply.
"What are you talking about?"

"Mrs. Ireland, Mrs. Ireland!"

"No one named Mrs. Ireland was involved.
No one else was hurt at all. Just Laura Hope.
Now calm down and tell me what you're talking about. Who's Mrs. Ireland and who's Joey,
and what were you doing with them?"

I had to be sure. "I'll call you back," I said,
and hung up.

Mrs. Ireland answered her phone on the first
ring. She was obviously all right, so I hung up
without speaking. I'd explain later.

Sam was not pleased with me when I got
back to him and explained what, where, and
who. When we finally got it sorted out it was
appallingly clear that Laura had been attacked
within minutes of my seeing her drive away.

When we returned from our Space Needle
dinner Laura had let all three of us out in front
of the apartment and had then driven on around
the building to Sara's allotted parking space at

the back of the complex. I asked Mrs. Ireland if she would like Joey to see her to her door, but she said no, she was fine, and started up the walk to go inside. Joey and I went over to where I'd left the Toyota, got in, and left. I looked at my watch as I drove out onto the street. It read two minutes after seven.

"Is she going to be all right?" I asked.

"They don't know," Sam said, his voice harsh and tired. "She's in surgery right now. Something to do with her spine."

"When did you hear?"

"A couple of hours ago. She didn't have any identification on her so it took sometime to find out who she was."

"But how did you...Are you sure it's Laura?"

"Reasonably sure. Although I would like either you or Anna Carmine to see her as soon as possible so we can be positive. We traced her through the car rental people—she still had the keys clutched in her hand—but we'd like to get in touch with her husband. Do you know where we can find him?"

"No, although his office should be able to tell you. I think Laura said he was going to be in New York all week."

"What office? Do you have the number?"

"No again. I just know it's in San Francisco. Maybe Anna Carmine knows. Sam, could he, Williams, give you any description of the mugger?"

"No, none. When he first realized something was wrong Laura was already down. The felon, facing the other way, was bent over with his arm raised to hit her again. When Williams laid on his horn and started racing toward them the guy simply scuttled off into the shrubbery without turning or straightening up, so he couldn't even say how tall he was. Although he did say he had the impression the man was taller than the average."

"Sam, it doesn't sound like a mugging."

"I never said it was, but do you know of any reason why someone would want to hurt her? Kill her even? Or any connection to the Electric Toy Company other than the obvious?"

I didn't tell him that an hour ago I had almost convinced myself she was responsible for the two killings the Electric Toy Company had already sustained.

"No, not really, but I don't believe it was a mugger either."

After we hung up I sat trying again to put

the pieces together in my head but nothing wanted to gel.

If Carl Werner had been killed so that the three women could inherit the toy company, why had Sara been killed at practically the same time?

For Connie and Jean's benefit, so that they would be sole owners? Simply too farfetched to even consider. Neither woman fit any kind of criminal profile.

So that Laura would own Sara's share? Very tricky. If it hadn't been for Sara's call to me, the time of her death might still be in doubt. Laura might never have inherited. The case could have been tied up in the courts for years. Anna was a very careful lawyer.

I thought about that for a while, and about Laura being attacked. The attack bothered me. Sara's allotted space was at the very back of the lot next to a wide band of shrubbery. Not the sort of place the average mugger would choose to wait for a victim to come along. And the timing was wrong, too. Laura had let us off at almost exactly seven; Williams spotted her situation at seven-fifteen. It couldn't have taken her more than a minute to drive around the building. What had happened in that missing fourteen minutes? Had she gone someplace? Met someone?

I pushed that thought around for a time before I got up and walked over to the door. "Martha, does that friend of yours still work in the coroner's office?" I asked.

"Yes. What do you want?"

"See if she'll fax us a copy of the report on Sara's autopsy, will you?"

She called and a few minutes later the fax machine clicked into life.

Sara had died of a crushed larynx, which induced a laryngeal spasm causing almost instant suffocation. Not necessarily the same as being strangled.

And then it all fell into place. Like a jigsaw puzzle, once you place the pivotal piece, the rest is easy.

TWENTY-SIX

I PULLED UP Sara's file on my computer and set to work updating it. I seem to think more clearly when I can see my thoughts on the screen. Martha was on the phone in the other room. I couldn't hear what she was saying, but the sound distracted me. I got up and crossed the room, meaning to close the door, and heard Martha say, "I'm sorry, too, Borda, but I think you will be a lot better off regardless."

Borda? What in the world? I stood in the doorway listening until she hung up.

"How's that for smarts?" she said, giving me a smug smile.

"How in the heck did you find her?"

"Remember the cellular phone call on the Saturday morning Carl was killed? To his house?"

I nodded.

"I traced it easy enough. The number belonged to a Martin Berg. The name sounded faintly German, and remembering that Borda was German, I followed it up and finally got a hold of Borda a few minutes ago. Martin has a farm up by Monroe. He and Borda have been seeing each other, her words not mine, for over a year. That's where she was Saturday night. She locked Millard in his room a little after six o'clock and off she went.''

"Well, why didn't she say so?"

"Up until the morning you saw her she still thought she was going to inherit Carl's house and was afraid the police would think she had something to do with his death. She was afraid to leave because she thought that would disinherit her. She's not very bright. She was actually in the process of packing when you got there. She had talked to Anna earlier and knew she wasn't in his will at all.''

"Poor thing."

"Yes and no. I think she will be perfectly happy with her farmer and she says Millard loves the animals.''

"I'm glad for her."

I went back to my computer and was still figuring out ways and means when Martha called to me in a pleased voice. "Hey, Demary, I found the ten grand.''

"Where?" I went out to look over her shoulder.

"Look here." She pointed at the screen. "I discovered the toy company has three checking accounts in the bank. One, if you can believe this, is listed in the ETC chart of accounts as 'extraneous income' and that's where she entered the ten thou. And, as far as I can figure, she dropped the money in the night depository Friday night. I'll have to check with the bank, but I'm pretty sure that's it."

"Extraneous income? What kind of a cash account is that?"

"Nothing I've ever heard of before. Maybe it's supposed to be funny. I'm no accountant. The only thing I can tell you is that all of the deposits are ten thousand or less and they are small change compared to the other two accounts. Those toys generate an incredible amount of money. It costs plenty to produce them, but still…"

"Jeepers. I'd like to have that kind of cash flow."

"Wouldn't we all."

I WENT BACK TO my desk and the scheme I had conjured up, called Anna to be sure of my ground, tidied up some of the loose ends in my head, then went out to Martha again.

"You don't look well, Martha. You need a vacation," I told her in a solicitous tone.

"What?" She frowned at me. "Don't be silly. It was just the way the bloody twit told me about Laura that made me upchuck."

"Nope, you need a vacation, and I've got just the one. I want you to buy yourself a round-trip ticket to England to do some research for Mr. Robert Dudley. You will document every single thing you do, of course, including traveling to the Liverpool area where said prince visited. While you're there you can visit your relatives, have a good time, and when Dudley-slash-Sharin's twenty-five hundred dollars is gone, and you've spent at least another thousand, you can come home."

"Huh?" Her expression changed to delight as the idea sunk in.

"And when you get back we will send Mr. Dudley-slash-Sharin a very detailed and itemized statement of our services. No one can possibly complain because we will have done exactly what Mr. Robert Dudley asked us to do. At no time did I say *I* would make a trip to England personally."

We both started giggling. "Sharin will have a cow," Martha chortled. "I love it."

So did I. "Call our travel agent and book yourself a flight next week."

She picked up the phone and then put it down again. "Wait a minute. What about Sara? And Laura? What are you…"

I told her.

BACK IN MY OFFICE a bit later I was sorting out what I needed to do first when I had another phone call. It was Captain Tyson, calling to tell me that Jon North's *Pacific Dreamer* was back tied up at his slip down the dock from the *Shady Lady*.

"When did he get back?" I asked, picking up my purse as I spoke.

"Saturday evening, according to one of my friends here. I've been gone, went to see an old shipmate up in Bellingham, and didn't get back until late last night. If you want to talk…"

"I'll be down as soon as I can get there," I assured him. "But if you talk to him first don't tell him I'm looking for him."

"Not likely I would," he said dryly.

Shouting to Martha where I was going as I ran out the door, I jumped in the Toyota, and darned near got creamed by a pickup as I pulled away from the curb. It disappeared on down the street toward the U district before I had time to do more than hit the brakes. I'm not very knowledgeable about cars—I can't tell a Ford from a BMW—but this was definitely a pickup and it was painted a psychedelic blue.

Either the darn thing is following me around or there is a whole fleet of trucks painted that color blue, I thought angrily.

There was a ten-second lapse while I processed that thought, then one more piece dropped into place.

I had it all together now, or at least I thought I did, but I still didn't know what I was going to do about it. One thing I didn't have was proof. None. This killer had been very clever.

CAPTAIN TYSON WAS waiting for me in the parking lot near the slips.

"Thought maybe I'd just hang around, make sure things didn't get out of hand," he said as we walked toward the stairs leading down to the water. "You carrying a gun?"

"No," I said, blinking in surprise. I'd never even thought about bringing a gun. I have a .32 and I'm licensed but I never carry it. I don't like guns.

"S'alright," he said, giving me an easy smile. "I've got mine."

That stopped me in my tracks. He swung his jacket open to reveal an old navy issue sidearm that looked as big as a howitzer.

"Good grief! You can't... He isn't a serial killer, for heaven's sake. He's not dangerous."

"You don't know that. He's not a smart man, in fact, he's stupid, and a stupid man doesn't think, he acts, and that makes him dangerous," Tyson said, speaking as I realized later, from years of experience as a navy officer in charge of a diverse variety of seafarers.

"Well, pul-leese, don't go waving that cannon at him," I told him.

"You take care of your job, gal, I'll take care of mine," he said, nodding toward the dock below us. "There's your man."

He was about fifty feet ahead of us, just stepping off his boat onto the dock. Barefoot, dressed in cutoff jeans and a torn T-shirt, he had long, sun-bleached blond hair and moved with the smooth agility of a cat.

He was still tying up when Captain Tyson and I reached him. He looked up with a pleasant smile and a word to the captain and for a second I doubted my conclusions.

"Gal here wants to talk to you," Tyson said neutrally. "Name's Demary Jones."

"Hi, Demary. What about?" He finished with the rope and stepped back onto the *Dreamer* to toss a couple of more bumpers over the side before picking up a boat hook and stepping dockside again.

I opened my mouth to say something innocuous, something that would lead up to what I had in mind, but at the last second I looked into his brilliant green eyes, heard Sara's voice in my ear, and like a fool, I blurted it out.

"You didn't mean to kill her, did you?"

In the space of a heartbeat Sara's tall blond beachboy did an unbelievable Jekyll and Hyde into a feral creature with eyes like black holes.

I knew he was holding a potential weapon— that old boat hook was on a six-foot solid-oak pole—but even as I realized I'd made a bad mistake it didn't occur to me that he'd actually use it. There were a half-dozen people on the dock, plus Captain Tyson. I did see it coming when he swung but I couldn't dodge fast enough. The pole hit me across the shoulders with incredible force and I went flying. I knew I was going into the water and I tried to hold my breath. I didn't know I was going to hit an anchor chain on the way down.

I woke up in the hospital with a sore head, a broken arm, and everybody mad at me.

TWENTY-SEVEN

ONE MINUTE NOTHING, the next I was more or less awake, had a thundering headache, and remembered hearing the boom of Captain Tyson's big gun just before I hit the water.

"Tyson didn't kill him, did he?" I mumbled to the indistinct figure beside my bed. Jon North was my only hope of proving who killed whom and if Tyson had shot him I was well and truly out of luck.

"No, I certainly didn't, and not wanting to spend my golden years in a cell, I didn't even shoot *at* him," I heard Tyson say somewhat tartly.

"Not the way *I* heard it."

That was Sam's voice. What was he doing here in my bedroom? For that matter, what was Captain Tyson doing here?

I drifted off into a gray world where I didn't hurt.

When I floated to the surface again I realized I was lying on a gurney in a hospital examining room. My head still ached and the room was full of people.

Sam was there as well as Captain Tyson, Martha, a diminutive nurse, and a very young man in jeans and a T-shirt that I thought was an orderly. I was wrong about him. The very young man was a noted orthopedic surgeon.

Sam and he were talking, which gave Martha a chance to bawl me out before Sam got his innings in.

"You don't have good sense," Martha said acerbically, seeing my eyes open. "If nothing else you should have had the brains to stand far enough away from him so he couldn't hit you with the thing. You nearly got yourself killed."

"I had to use my sidearm. Almost cost me my permit," Captain Tyson said, not sounding a bit pleased with me either. He was standing on the other side of the gurney holding my hand. My good hand. The other hand, and entire arm, was swathed in some kind of armor plate. Or at least that was the way it felt.

"Your permit is for a World War II Navy souvenir, not a working .45," Sam snapped, abandoning the doctor. "How many times do I have to tell you, Demary, you can't…"

I moaned artistically and shut my eyes.

Thirty seconds later I was alone in the room except for the nurse. That adolescent-appearing doctor had a forceful personality.

The nurse held her cool little fingers on my wrist for a few moments, then said, "You can open your eyes. They're all gone. But I'm going to give you a light anesthetic now so Dr. Tray can work on your arm." She inserted a syringe into the drip attached to my shoulder somewhere.

"What's the matter with me?"

"Greenstick fracture of the ulna. Nothing serious. You got a whack on the head, a superficial cut on the forearm, and you inhaled a lot of dirty water. We have already aspirated most of that. As I said, nothing serious."

Maybe *she* didn't think any of it was serious. I did. I felt horrible. "Why is everybody so mad at me?" I asked. "I didn't sink his boat, did I?"

She smiled. "I think they are all fond of you."

"I'd rather have flowers," I grumbled, drifting off to sleep.

I SPENT A frustrating afternoon. Nobody knew anything about anything, except my hurts, of course, which grew less as the day wore on. Neither Sam nor Martha came back and as the several doctors who had taken over from the orthopedic man kept moving me from place to place for various poking and prodding, I couldn't even telephone. My right arm, from elbow to wrist, was encased in a canvaslike binding that was held together with sticky straps. I could take it off to shower, or scratch, and it didn't weigh much more than a cotton bandage. I was stiff and sore all over but the headache was fading to a dull ache behind my ear.

Despite my objections—I wanted to go home—the internist insisted on keeping me overnight. Something to do with the polluted water I'd swallowed and inhaled. A nurse installed me in a regulation hospital room with cool green walls and a regulation hard bed.

I was anxious to use the phone, to find out what had happened, but before I could sit up and reach for it Martha came in. She must have been waiting in the hall somewhere.

"You are looking considerably better," she said, leaning down to give me a gentle hug. "How do you feel?"

"About ready to climb the walls. What happened? Nobody around here knows a thing. What happened with Jon North? Did he admit killing Sara? Did they catch him? Did he try to get away? Did he…''

''Whoa. Give me a chance,'' she said. Smiling, she pulled the chair up to the bed and sat down beside me. ''North didn't even try to get away. Actually, he couldn't very well. Captain Tyson had a gun stuck in his ear.''

''You were there?''

''I called Sam—luckily he was at his desk—told him where you'd run off to, and followed you out the door. I was getting out of the car in the parking lot when the captain fired in the air. Nearly fainted, I did. I thought North had shot you.''

''Aw, I didn't know you cared,'' I said, grinning at her.

She gave me an exasperated look. ''Silly me.''

''Well, then what happened?''

''I'm not sure. By the time I got to the stairs Tyson had North facedown on the dock, and, as I said, had his gun stuck in the man's ear. A couple of other men were in the water holding you afloat and a couple more were helping get you out. You were still in the water when Sam got there." She paused, looking thoughtful. "You know, maybe you ought to marry him, Demary. He was certainly concerned enough about you. He might make a good husband after all."

I think my mouth fell open.

She shrugged. "Maybe not. He got over it in a hurry and spent most of the time in emergency swearing."

"Well, did North confess? Did he tell who and why?"

"If he did I don't know about it. Sam charged him with assault and had him taken off to the nick and that's the last I know about him. Captain Tyson and I followed you and Sam to the emergency room. When the doctor kicked us out I went back to the office, closed up, and came back here to see how you were."

Martha stayed until visiting hours were over and although I called Sam three times and left my number, he never called back. I was so mad at him by the time I went to sleep it was a wonder I didn't run a temperature.

I WOKE UP the next morning feeling well enough to be hungry and was reaching for the call button when the door opened to admit a tall, good-looking man in a white coat with kinky-curly blond hair. The nurse who followed on his heels gave him a puzzled glance as she came over to check my pulse. He nodded at her, turned, and started back out of the room before my still sleep-fuzzed brain registered who he was.

"That's David Hope!" I yelled, struggling to sit up. "Don't let him get away. He killed Carl!" Which, as stupid moves go, should certainly rank right up there with the best.

David whipped around like an adagio dancer, hitting the nurse across the side of her head with a forearm blow that slammed her sideways and into the bedside stand. It went over with a crash.

Screaming at the top of my lungs, I tumbled out, and under, the bed. Unless he had a gun he was going to have to scramble around on the floor to reach me, considerably evening the odds.

He didn't try. Instead he turned, jerked open the door, and ran full tilt into a solid phalanx of nurses, all trying to get through the door at once. Sam, at the head of the group, connected with a right to the jaw that by sheer good luck

put David on the floor in exactly the right position for me to administer the coup de grace.

My bare foot didn't do as much damage as I
would have liked, but he didn't offer much re-
sistance when Sam jerked his wrists behind him
and applied nylon cuffs.

It took some time to get everything sorted out
and David Hope on his way to the pokey. Eventually, however, things calmed down, I got my
discharge papers, and Sam took me home. He
deposited me on one of the two silk upholstered
love seats I have in front of the fireplace, gave
me a quick kiss, and went upstairs to make a
pot of tea.

It felt good to be home, and so did the kiss.
Maybe I ought to think about marrying him at
that.

"How long have you known it was David
Hope who killed Carl?" I asked when he came
back with teapot and cups and put them down
on the old chest I use as a coffee table.

"Since about the time you went charging off
after Jon North. Laura regained consciousness
for a while that morning. I had Carol Ann Guginsberg standing by. Laura told her David was
waiting for her in the parking lot. Apparently

she had told him she was filing for a divorce and he tried to talk her out of it.''

"I didn't think she really meant to do it."

"I guess he didn't either, not to start with anyway. When he finally did realize she meant it he told her he hadn't gone to the trouble of killing Carl and Sara to have her ruin his plans by getting a divorce.''

"What a horrible thing to say! Besides, if he had that stocking with him he meant to kill her."

"I think the DA will go for premeditated, all right. And I believe he will be tried for Laura's murder rather than for Carl's.''

"What else did she... Wha-at? What did you say? Laura's murder? Laura isn't...''

Sam put a comforting arm around my shoulder.

"Sam?" My voice cracked.

"I'm sorry, Demary. Laura was only conscious for a few minutes. She died an hour later.''

"Oh, no. Oh, Sam, why? Why did he do it? Surely not just for the money. What did he say?" Tears trickled down my face. Sam wiped them off with his thumb.

"He didn't say a word, and he already had a

high-priced lawyer lined up, so he won't be saying anything in the future either. Doesn't matter though. We have Laura's voice on tape identifying him and it was undoubtedly for the money. He's in serious financial trouble, facing bankruptcy for sure and possible criminal charges as well. He knew the toy company had an enormous cash flow and he probably figured he could steal enough from it to cover his losses without anyone ever catching him. But first Laura had to inherit, and for that to happen both Carl and then Sara had to die.''

"But how did he ever get Carl to let him in that night?''

"He was waiting for him, parked in his driveway in that blue truck. He had stolen the truck the day before because he didn't want to chance anyone seeing his cart here at that hour of the morning. When he saw Carl coming down the street he got out and stood alongside the hood looking as innocent as possible, I'm sure. According to North, David was going to tell Carl something about one of his toys that would somehow get him in the house and I guess it must have worked.''

"Was he the hit-and-run that bashed Connie?''

"We think so, and if your little pal Joey can ID the truck we'll nail him for that, too."

"Do you think he meant to kill all of them? Sara and Jean and Connie?"

"He may have. He's certainly about as cold-blooded a guy as I've run across in a long time."

I showed him the picture I'd taken of Carol Ann leaning against the railing on Jake's boat, with the *Pacific Dreamer* in the background and the very recognizable shape of the big Shilshole Bay breakwater in the distance. Timed and dated late Saturday afternoon, the snap showed North still just outside the locks long after he claimed to have been in the San Juan Islands. Which, by itself, didn't actually prove much of anything but it had set me thinking, and when I remembered the picture of David that had fallen out of Laura's purse and matched it to the one of him and North that Captain Tyson had given me, most of my bits and pieces suddenly fit together.

As the old saying goes, when you've eliminated all the possibles, the impossible must be right. *Que bono?* David Hope.

"What did North tell you about Sara?" I asked.

"Everything he knows and then some. He's trying to cop a lesser charge, of course. He swears he didn't mean to kill her. And you were right, she wasn't meant to die that morning. The plan was for North to get her on his boat, make sure she was seen, but always from a distance so she couldn't call for help, and head for the Pacific. Once they were sufficiently far offshore he was supposed to drop her overboard and send out an SOS call."

"How beastly!"

"And it could have worked. He doesn't have any kind of a record, not even juvenile, and no visible motive, so murder would have been hard to prove. If we'd even thought of it. Now of course he says he never would have killed her. Says he would have brought her back safe and sound."

I shuddered, wondering if he'd told Sara what he'd intended.

Sam read my thoughts. "He told her what David intended. That's how he got her into his car. Told her he'd never do anything like that and instead he'd take her to the closest police station where he'd help her swear out a warrant for David's arrest."

"How did he and David ever get together?"

"Born that way. They're distant relatives. His mother and David's mother are second cousins. He, North, says David has been getting him into trouble ever since they were kids, but he never meant to go along with this."

"Ha. I don't believe that. I'll bet David promised him enough money to buy the big new boat he wants."

"Very likely, and that's where his story breaks down. He could have gone to the police any time, on his own. And if he was taking her to file a complaint, why, as he claims, would she suddenly start screaming she wanted out of the car? That's when he says he grabbed at her to keep her from jumping out in the middle of the freeway and 'accidentally' got her across the throat with his forearm."

"Actually, that part is possible. Especially with a woman as small as Sara. If he happened to hit her right across her larynx it could have happened."

"So he says. Then he panicked and left her in that garage. If he'd got her out of the apartment in the middle of the night as he was supposed to have done—David had supplied him with a key—very possibly her death would have gone down as the accident David planned. Instead the whole scheme collapsed.''

"So why did he wait till morning?''

"He overslept.''

THE BEST laid plans...

MARY LOGUE

DARK

COULEE

A CLAIRE WATKINS MYSTERY

Though life in rural Wisconsin is having some healing effects for ex-Minneapolis cop Claire Watkins, she is still plagued by nightmares of past tragedy. Now she's plunged into a shattering murder case that will force her to confront the demons that still haunt her.

Widower Jeb Spitzer is knifed to death at the local harvest moon dance, leaving three teenagers orphaned. But Claire senses a feeling of desperate relief among the three kids. As she peels back the layers of the crime, she uncovers a shocking connection to Spitzer's wife's "accidental" death, and secrets that premeditated both incidents.

Available October 2001
at your favorite retail outlet.

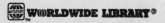

WML398

Kathleen Anne Barrett

Milwaukee
Autumns
Can Be
LETHAL

A BETH HARTLEY MYSTERY

Lawyer turned legal researcher and amateur
sleuth, Beth Hartley is hired to do some
work for an old law school acquaintance,
Don Balstrum. But when she finds Don
murdered in his office, her meticulous
mind for details leads her immediately
on the path of a complex crime.

With her tenacity and insight into
the legal profession, she soon opens
many dark doors into Don's world: his
unforgiving father, his antagonistic twin
brother, his cagey business partners and
his ex-wife—all with secrets to hide.

Available October 2001 at your favorite retail outlet.

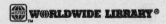 **WORLDWIDE LIBRARY®**

WKAB399

Camille Minichino

The Beryllium Murder

A GLORIA LAMERINO MYSTERY

Physicist-sleuth Gloria Lamerino heads back to her old stomping grounds in Berkeley, California, to look into the death of a former colleague, Gary Larkin, dead of beryllium poisoning. Though his death has been ruled accidental, Gloria is suspicious: Gary was much too aware of the hazards of this dangerous element to be so reckless in his handling of it.

The pieces of the puzzle come together like a new molecular formula for homicide: Internet pornography, hacking, extortion, jealousy and revenge—and a killer making murder into a science.

"It's a good thing the periodic table is big enough for 100 more adventures."
—Janet Evanovich, author of *Hot Six*

Available October 2001 at your favorite retail outlet.

Take 2 books and a surprise gift FREE!

SPECIAL LIMITED-TIME OFFER

Enjoy the mystery and suspense of

POISON APPLES

NANCY MEANS WRIGHT

A VERMONT MYSTERY

"Wright's most gripping and satisfying mystery to date."
—*Female Detective*

"…Wright doesn't put a foot wrong in this well-wrought mystery."
—*Boston Globe*

After tragedy shatters Moira and Stan Earthrowl's lives, running an apple orchard in Vermont gives them a chance to heal. Yet their newfound idyll is short-lived as "accidents" begin to plague the massive orchard: tractor brakes fail, apples are poisoned.

Desperate, Moira turns to neighbor Ruth Willmarth for help. Ruth's investigation reveals a list of possible saboteurs, including a fanatical religious cult and a savvy land developer who, ironically, is Ruth's ex-husband. But deadly warnings make it clear that even Ruth is not immune to the encroaching danger….